Welcome to Winterberry High

by

Fabian Grant

Paperback edition first published in the United Kingdom in 2019 by aSys Publishing

eBook edition first published in the United Kingdom in 2019 by aSys Publishing

A CIP catalogue record for this book is available from the British Library.

ISBN: 978-1-07-450346-8

aSys Publishing 2019

http://www.asys-publishing.co.uk

Contents

For those of you having a bad day and yet you still try
Please spare a thought for Oscar Smart down at
Winterberry High

CHAPTER 1

Sugar Nation

'Open wide Oscar. Make sure you lick it. Try to get the full effect of the flavours,' said Mr Sugar.

Six gentlemen, suited and booted, longingly awaited my judgement.

Please don't be alarmed; allow me a formal introduction. I was an ordinary boy living an ordinary life. So far, I've had a deliriously entertaining childhood. My complaints are fairly modest in comparison to poor kids.

When I'm not educating myself at Diamond Division School for boys, the best in the country (not bragging just stating facts), you'll locate me at home, probably driving my petrol-powered remote-control car. If Timothy, an equally privileged child was home, we'd chill in his tree house. I say tree house; however, two bedrooms, fully furnished, thick fluffy cream carpets and indoor heating aren't typical. Timothy doesn't do swinging tyres, too much exercise. On a few occasions, father would surprise me with trips to the most exotic and exclusive locations. I've seen the Great Wall of China, the Eiffel Tower in Paris, the wonderful pyramids in Egypt and New York's Statue of Liberty.

I'm starting to paint a beautiful picture. Life is a piece of lemon cheesecake (a favourite of mine). But the purpose isn't for me to flaunt my vast empire in front of the less fortunate.

Before you jump to conclusions, don't suggest for a millisecond that I'm some spoilt rich kid. Instilled in me is the mentality we work hard, we play hard. From the tender age of eight, I've worked to earn my keep. I take my job very seriously. In fact, some consider me to have the premiere role in my company. I tap into a market they'd be oblivious to at Sugar Nation.

Sugar Nation is the largest distributors of sweets and chocolate in the universe. And, lucky for me, I was chief taster. Researchers say that one in five sweets consumed in the world is made by Sugar Nation's great staff. Who gives them the seal of approval? Me.

Being a sweet kingpin created a mystique around me. All the children from the block rushed to ask me about what would be entering the market next. 'Are they coming out with chocolate pop, fizzy yet thick?' enquired one child. 'Chocolate bubble gum would be cool,' glowed another kid. 'No, chicken flavoured bubble gum.'

'You'll have to wait and see,' I'd tell them, putting my finger to my nose.

With the great power I garnered through my career status, it meant I could be very selective in choosing friends. I ranked them in three separate categories. One, looks; no funny looking friends. That ruled out bug-eyed Burt and big head Callum. Two, riches; this is how Timothy became my top guy. Hey, you've never slept over in his tree house. And three, envy. If a person doesn't feel jealous of me and how I live, then they're not worth knowing, right?

How did I land a job so cushy? Well, daddy is managing director. Not sure if that had something to do with it. The first Saturday in each month was marked in my personal business planner as "tasty time". And at 8am, while almost all children are snuggled up in bed, me and daddio wolfed down a power breakfast then headed out. Father and son on the open highway, racing to a professional meeting, is the stuff of dreams.

Sitting in the passenger seat reading the business sector, I felt so official. Dad was a well-to-do fella, always clean shaven. Even on a day off he'd be seen wearing a suit. His hair glistened with several expensive hair care products and a side parting. The shoes were Italian leather fresh from the catwalks in Milan. I idolised him and tried to mimic him in every situation. 'Oscar, I need your A-game today,' said dad.

'I'll give it my all,' I replied.

'Be honest. I can't reiterate how valuable your input is.' There was a serious side to the tone he used.

'I'm always on the money. I'm a well-seasoned professional.'

'Just checking you're in supreme shape.'

'After three years I got this down to a science, dad,' I boasted.

He never usually pestered about my work. I sensed an extraordinary level of stress hampering his character. And his nerves transmitted nerves to me. I began to second-guess my skills, adding an intense amount of pressure. The car seat became hard, its seatbelt pinning me in.

'Why is today so vital?' I wondered.

Dad puffed out his cheeks and clutched the steering wheel a little hard. 'We've got some rivals in the form of Candy Planet.'

'So? Aren't Sugar Nation the world's biggest manufacturers of sweets?'

'Yes, and we'd like to keep it that way.'

'How much of a threat does Candy Planet pose?'

Dad gripped the steering wheel even more imposingly. 'Over the past six months they've eaten chunks out of our profits.'

My throat clammed up a bit hearing this shocking revelation. Competition for a juggernaut such as Sugar Nation startled me. 'We're gonna fight back, right dad?' I said.

'Of course we are. Candy Planet is in for a world of pain. I'm gonna take utter satisfaction in running them into the ground,' dad fumed, punching the dashboard.

There was a ruthless streak about his intentions for rival sweet producers. Father always appeared calm, a gentle soul. He'd help an old lady across the street, retrieve a kite from a tree. However, in the heat of a boardroom, the man switched into a monster.

'Aren't there enough children for us and Candy Planet to prosper?'

His silence frightened me. For the rest of the journey, we were uncomfortable in each other's presence. As we approached the skyscraper life seemed disjointed, the joyous experience of chief taster crumbling.

The glass elevator that surged us up to the executive suite was out of order. An ominous sign by anybody's standards. Sixty-two flights of stairs pushed me to my deepest limits as my chunky thighs rubbed together. The boardroom normally had a laidback, chilled-out vibe. Sadly, Candy Planet had corroded the cheery atmosphere.

You know it's significant when owner Mr Sugar arrives. He built his company from sugar, obviously, and a limitless imagination. Mr Sugar grew up dirt poor in the 50s. England was beginning to rebuild after the end of World War 2 in 1945. Upon his dad's return, things were a struggle; they survived on food rations or friends and neighbours' castoffs. Luxury to Mr Sugar could be a slice of wholemeal bread. Sometimes his dad worked three jobs to see them through the harshest times. Their lifestyle never altered; work, sleep and pay bills. That's all he saw of his father. It wasn't until Mr Sugar's cousin's wedding that he originally tasted sherbet. The magical candy fizzed and popped inside his mouth. 'What is this marvellous food?' he asked.

'Sweets. Don't tell me you've never had a sweet before?' replied his cousin.

Mr Sugar embarrassingly shrugged.

'Cousin, you've got a lot to eat up on.'

His little cousin smiled, ushering Mr Sugar toward the children's section. On the table a large and magnificent bowl crammed with jelly babies, cola bottles, liquorice allsorts and a few hard-boiled sweets sat engagingly.

'Wowzer,' screamed Mr Sugar.

The rainbow coloured candy dazzled, aided by the disco lights.

'Is this for us?' hoped Mr Sugar as his hand neared the bowl.

'You betcha.'

Mr Sugar launched both hands deep into the bowl, lining his pockets before he woke up from his perfect dream. He rapidly bit the packaging off, shovelling in sweet after sweet. Candy after candy jolted his body in excitement.

'Enjoy yourself; no one's gonna take it away from you.'

'Are you serious?'

His cousin nodded, giving Mr Sugar a spark that carried and ignited his entrepreneurial spirit.

'Yes. Not only that, there are shops where you can buy this.'

They say you'll never forget your first piece of confectionery. Those couple of hours transformed Mr Sugar's landscape for eternity. On his return home, the remaining chocolates and sweets he took to school. Kids surrounded him adoringly. The playground became his very own tuck shop; children pooled their money together, buying sweets for a shilling. Within the space of a year a thirteen-year-old Mr Sugar was making as much money as his father. In the holidays, he'd set up a stall outside his poverty-rav-aged home.

After his schooldays were behind him, he began working for himself full-time. Sugar Nation was born from a relatively humble start. But one afternoon, as the sun shone extravagantly through his shop window, he witnessed a blessing in disguise. The heat melted his hard-boiled candy, making them sticky.

'What a jam! If only there was a way to keep the shell hard and inside sticky,' he said curiously.

He pondered for months if such a creation could be achieved. A handful of major fails later "The Sugar surprise" arrived, making Mr Sugar a fat bundle. Invention on top of invention appeared, including chewing gum toothpaste, which is the equivalent of brushing your teeth. My dentist swears by it. Once Sugar Nation established itself as a household name, Mr Sugar shunned the spotlight, letting new blood run his vast portfolio.

So, if he ever came off the golf course long enough, every employee scurried around as if they were on ice skates.

'Is the bottled water at room temperature? Did everyone get their brief on words to avoid?' panicked the C.E.O, knowing his neck was on the line.

'Oh bugger, I forgot to send the email,' announced his secretary.

The C.E.O chuckled in a profound way, holding his head down. 'She forgot to send the email. She forgot to send the email. She forgot to send the email!' Every time he repeated the sentence his volume increased.

'I'd lose my head if it wasn't screwed on. Shall I print them out?'

'Don't bother, he stared at the young lady, a malicious smirk drove across his face. 'It's with great pleasure that I inform you – you're fired!'

His secretary's face fell, and she took a trip to teary-land. 'Sir, it was an accident,' she wept.

'Get out. Leave your I.D necklace at reception,' said the C.E.O with zero empathy.

'How am I gonna support my kids?' She blew her nose as her face reddened. 'Their father died saving orphans from a burning building.'

'Tell your sob story to someone who gives a damn.'

I'd never seen how cutthroat business could be until then.

The bewildered secretary packed up her desk.

'Right, now that's out of the way I feel fantastic.'

'How are we gonna know what words and topics to avoid?' asked dad.

The C.E.O began to sweat profusely; buckets flopped off his head. 'Avoid using negative language. Anything like decreased units sold, loss of earnings and, whatever happens, never mention Candy Planet's resurgence.'

As the word Candy Planet floated from his lips, the boardroom door flashed open. 'What is this about Candy Planet?' ordered Mr Sugar.

Mr Sugar stormed through the office like a tornado. Bigwig executives sat gripped with fear like children summoned by the principal.

'We were saying how they'll be ruing the day they decided to enter our domain,' suggested the C.E.O.

'Good to know I've got soldiers wired for war,' Mr Sugar was a no-nonsense sort of guy. His big broad shoulders were a platform for a head that only held one expression; success, success and more success.

'Bang bang baby!' The C.E.O blew smoke off the gun he made with his hand.

'Display the new invention that'll bury Candy Planet.'

We all gasped for oxygen, as if a vacuum had sucked out all the air. 'Unveil the Cube of Consequence.'

My turn in the hotseat came around swiftly. The Cube of Consequence split into four layers, each representing a new flavour or texture. The multi-coloured sweet's colours spiralled together depending on how the light hit it.

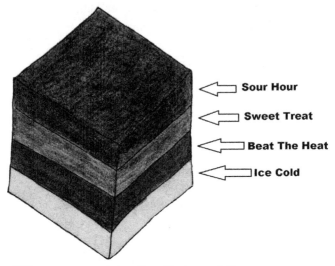

'What are we waiting for, Christmas? Eat young man, eat,' barked Mr Sugar.

I trembled a little; nobody ever spoke to me with such velocity. As I popped the sweet in my mouth, weird emotions disrupted my usual routine. However, instantly I was blown away by a sour kick which my eyeballs are yet to recover from. After section one, a killing wave of sickly sugar sent me cuckoo. Section three came with fire; imagine dipping your tongue in gasoline then striking a match. And finally, fourth brought its ice; now attempt eating fifty giant ice cubes, brain freeze. As I finally got to grips with this disgusting sweet, it dissolved into my tongue.

'Well young man, what's your opinion?' rushed Mr Sugar.

I'd barely swallowed before he ambushed me.

Numerous executives' faces turned blue from their lack of breathing.

'Um, it's so delicious,' I replied, not completely sold.

Mr Sugar's vicious green eyes lightened. 'He likes it.'

The mood in the room elevated to one of harmony.

'Well done, Oscar,' said the very relieved C.E.O, shaking my hand.

'Splendid. We'll go to market Monday. That'll cut Candy Planet down a peg or two,' insisted Mr Sugar, stroking his glossy silver locks.

In life, one should have patience, because jumping the gun can result in an epic disaster.

CHAPTER 2

The Tongue

Following another successful evaluation on my behalf, mother, father and I would go out for a bite to eat. Pizza Perfection sells the greatest pizza in human history – forget what you've heard – and was always my no.1 choice. It enabled me to be creative and experiment with a variety of toppings. Their dough was fresh and puffy. I'd take a moment when entering the restaurant to hover near the kitchen just to get a whiff of the alluring smell. I'm gonna eat pizza until it comes out my ears.

Pizza Perfection had a traditional stone bake oven, and the building was painted in green, white and red to represent its Italian heritage.

'So how was work?' asked mom.

'Good. Just another day at the office,' I said. Unfortunately, my stomach didn't get the memo as I began to get this queasy feeling.

'Oscar delivered a career-best performance in there,' praised dad.

Always nice to get the seal of approval from a loved one. Too bad my tummy's having fits.

Maybe a glass of coke would soothe this sudden bout of belly bother. No chance; I gulped down a whole bottle, only adding fuel to burning guts.

'Oh, what shall I have?' Mother could be so indecisive picking an outfit to wear, whether she wanted her hair up or down, and parking? Don't get me started. We'd have to leave home half an hour early if she drove. Dad always referred to it as women drivers. Not sure I entirely agree.

'I'm gonna treat myself with super cheesy cheese, extra spicy sausage, ham, pineapple and mushrooms.'

'Get anchovies and onions,' added mom; scanning the menu her faced beamed at the possibilities.

'Chicken, garlic and crispy bacon,' considered dad.

'You've got to stuff the crust. Steaming, gooey, melting cheese seeping out of every slice.'

As they continued to shift through the endless range of toppings, it compounded my worries.

'Oscar, you're very quiet,' said mom.

'Just a little jaded,' I rapidly answered, applying pressure to my tummy.

I averted my eyes away from hers. Mothers have this sixth sense when their child isn't honest.

Grrrrr! Grrrrr! Grrrr!

'Did you guys hear that?'

'Hear what? I think your ears need cleaning dad.'

Dad stared in my direction in earnest, as though he'd solved the mystery. 'Oscar, your face looks swollen. Are you sure you're not a little under the weather?' said dad caringly

'I'm in blinding condition, a hundred and ten per cent.' Maybe my star jumps were a tad extreme.

'Sit down, action man. Stop acting peculiar, son.' Mom yanked my arm.

I couldn't control my agony anymore; these stomach cramps began evolving. All the surrounding tables had giddy children scoffing their weight in pizza. The greasy, stringy, yellow mountains of cheese slopped about their rotating mouths. I could see their jaws clamping and chopping, absolute disgusting. They spat undigested meat onto adjoining tables as they attempted to speak

11

with a full mouth. Where's their class? Also, the adults stacked plates of towering pizza, devouring them like prisoners coming off a 30-day hunger strike.

'I'm not feeling pizza tonight. Ssstick to ssside sssalad.'

Mom placed the menu on the table her concern ramped up. 'Come again?'

'Gonna ssstick to ssside sssalad.' Inexplicably my tongue had outgrown my mouth, skimming my teeth whenever I spoke.

Father was an all-round prankster. So, he saw the amusing side of my inability to form S's. 'Say, simple sausages sound scrumptious sitting sizzling.'

'Leave it out,' instructed mom. However, her disturbed frown, along with longing sighs, ended all speculation. I must be messed up.

As waiters came back and forth through the kitchen's revolving door, they froze, leered at me, then ran to tell other employees. Dozens of chefs and waiters rushed to gawk at this medical freak.

'Oh, my giddy aunt, your neck,' screamed mom, her head wobbling in terror.

'Quick, I'll call the paramedics. Oscar, hang tight, it'll all be fine. Daddy guarantees it.'

People dropped knives and forks, reacting to the melee.

My neck expanded like a blowfish; it gradually engulfed my chin.

Jubilant children recorded videos of "exploding boy" on their camera phones. I'm going viral folks; by nightfall I'll have a million hits and be an A-lister.

Between tongue, neck and stomach I can honestly say I've had better days.

Six minutes later emergency services whisked me to A&E. Mom kept me company, holding my hand and kissing it repeatedly. She sang a soothing tune as they wheeled me to the operating rooms.

I lay in a hospital gown, agitated. Patients were being rolled here, there and everywhere. Some exhibited pleasant smiles, returning from a successful op, while other patients hollered, cried and bawled heading towards those ever so faithful double doors.

Having the financial prowess father has, I needn't fret. The private, highly qualified doctors and nurses meant I was in safe hands.

In the corridor, I heard a few medics chatting over my chart.

'This boy needs immediate surgery; his face is four times the original size,' said the doctor.

'Go ahead. We don't want another patient exploding, do we?' replied a nurse.

'Yes, once was bad enough, the second time a silly accident. But a third would highlight some imperfection in our abilities.'

'Been a while since you've done surgery, hasn't it?' said the nurse, a bit rattled.

'Forty-one years. No time like the present though.'

'Do you feel up to it?'

'Sure. Inject him, drain the excess fluid. Patch him back up and send him home,' he said casually.

My heart thudded, petrified. I started to undo the string gown, preparing to scale the hospital walls

'Ah, Oscar, I'll have you back on peak performance in a jiffy,' grinned the senior doctor. He was old, really old; old enough to remember carrier pigeons and dial-up internet. His rusty knees and joints buckled as he dawdled forwards; lifeless skin jiggled on his face.

'Doctor, I'm miles better now,' I persisted.

He pulled down his glasses, resting them on the tip of his triangular nose. This was supposed to be a reassuring moment, but his old worn out eyes and trembling hands only tripled my hesitation levels. 'Listen, Oscar, life calls upon the brave to handle a task most people are terrified of.' The doctor's speech seemed weak and forced.

'What ssssort of ssssurgery do I require?' damn you *s*.

The doctor ruffled through a medical bag, bringing out a stethoscope. He stood puzzled at the instrument.

13

'They go in your ears, doctor,' explained the nurse.

His bedside manner was appalling. He slung the thermometer into my gaping mouth and then, with hands made out of ice, pressed the stethoscope against my chest. 'Can you breathe out for me, lad?'

'Your hands are freezing,' I said, shuddering.

'Everything looks functional,' he informed the nurse.

'What's the procedure?' I wondered.

'It's your lucky day. Surgery isn't necessary.'

Relief, joy, serenity and peace lifted my soul.

'You've had a very serious allergic reaction. Have you eaten anything new in your diet?' guessed the doctor, placing two latex gloves on his bony hands.

Let me think, is there anything I have eaten recently that may have caused my ailment? I ate breakfast, lunch and no dinner, nothing untoward by anyone's books.

I sat up on the gurney, reviewing my food consumption.

'No doctor, I've got a steady meal plan.'

Mom and dad waited patiently in the room, stricken with guilt.

'Maybe your parents could share any additional information.'

'He's a regular child, nothing out the ordinary,' stated dad.

'Plan and simple average Oscar,' said mom.

Parents say it as they see it.

'Very well,' the wrinkle-faced doctor grabbed a humongous needle, draining one pint of fluid out of my swollen tongue.

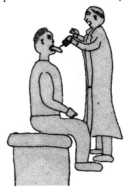

He wrote out a prescription for some medicine, which I'm to take twice daily until natural order is restored, and told me no solid foods for twenty-four hours, to add insult to injury.

CHAPTER 3

The D-word

Over the course of the weekend, my tongue healed nicely, and my *s*'s came back into action. I made up for lost time in the food department. I'm glad too, because the coming week was to be critical for me and my exquisite lifestyle. Firstly, being eleven meant I'd be leaving Diamond Division School for the best boys' school in the country. Did I mention that previously? Well, it's worth another shameless plug. Primary school has given me fantastic memories I'll cherish forever. But time goes by, and new undiscovered memories await Timothy and me at Platinum Grammar School of excellence – of excellence. And furthermore, Sugar Nation will launch "The Cube of Consequence", available at your local convenience store Monday.

Sunday night's sleep came with a heightened sense of anticipation. The moon rose to prominence, guarding its adoring stars; slender beams floated through my bedroom curtain. Any time Sugar Nation readied for a big promotional launch; dad worked every hour God sends. And we had been through some biggies like the Sludge Fudge Delight of 2011, and last year's Rainbow Bar yet another best seller.

The Cube of Consequence had been in the pipeline for eight months. This sweet was predicted to hammer the final nail in Candy Planet's coffin. I'd bought into my father's corporate mindset: crush, kill and destroy. The apple doesn't fall far from the tree.

**

Monday morning came around swiftly and brushed away the night sky. 'Rise and shine, Oscar,' yelled mom.

Oh, these early mom starts; when I rule the world, no one will be allowed to wake up before midday. Who's with me? 'Oscar, don't make me come up there.'

'Coming, mom,' I groggily responded, wiping sleep from the corner of my eyes.

As I prepared for school, a sincere sadness crept onto my back. The olive-green knee-high socks and blazers now didn't appear so ridiculous. I'm still not sold on the straw hat though. Schooldays supposedly are the best of your life. So, it's an absolute sin if you don't soak in the youthful excitement.

Sometimes, if the weather smiled down on us, Timothy and I would walk to school.

'Hey Oscar, look, my beard is coming through,' boasted Timothy.

Timothy was a heavy-set child with a rather large bum chin. His grey shorts would ride up his backside, giving him a constant wedgie. He had already lost two out of the three buttons that fought to close his blazer.

'My dad said I'll be able to shave soon too.'

Staring at Timothy's plump face, I noticed a faint tinge gracing his top lip.

'Pump the brakes, I can barely see it.'

Timothy tilted his head back, blocking out the sun.

'Take a gander at my astounding facial hair.'

I squinted, getting super close. That's when I recognised the lengths Timothy would go to impress me. I nudge the beard – I say that lightly – with my finger.

'Stop, you'll smudge it,' he squirmed.

'Beards don't smudge,' I chuckled.

Timothy played ignorant. 'My father said it is how they grow in first; takes two months before maximum effect.'

OK. He stuck to the script of lies forever. To give substance to his stories he always began with daddy told me this and father told me that, like adults know everything.

We carried on plodding toward Diamond Division. Before reaching the school, lately we'd taken the long route to pass Platinum Grammar School, observing the teenagers entering through the silver gated entrance.

'This September, Oscar, we'll be rolling up to those gates, cruising to lessons.'

Timothy and I envisioned us as the two stocky, handsome adolescents with expertly crafted goatees we'd later become.

'We're gonna run this place like stars,' I dreamed.

Platinum Grammar School was the biggest private school in Europe. It used to be a castle, but due to legal issues and the beheading of the former owner, it was renovated and opened as a secondary school. Eight hundred of the most intelligent and sophisticated kids flow through this institution each year.

'I can't wait to make the croquet and cricket team,' said Timothy.

We high-fived, ecstatic; for now, our aspirations were put on hold. There's nine weeks until September, and anything can and will go astray. I sailed through the school day unaware of what troubles were brewing on the home front.

After school, I jogged to my house (jogged = fast walk). As we grow up responsibilities come thick and fast. Before you know it, you're spreading your wings, so as I'm about to join secondary school mother trusted me with a key. It's a key moment in anyone's life. When I opened the door, dad had a gloomy expression. Here's a man that regularly used cucumber face scrubs and chemical peels now sat dumbstruck with bags gathered beneath his eyes big enough to hold elephants. 'Home early, aren't you?' I asked in surprise.

He kept his bewildered focus. 'Did you say something, Oscar?'

'Doesn't matter,' I wandered upstairs. The burden and stress both parents lived under intimidated me.

Days came and went, and dad's tension grew; pressure at work left him drained. Apparently, The Cube didn't revolutionise the confectionery world as anticipated. Sales plummeted and plummeted. A reduction in price couldn't shift units. Buy one get one free, forget about it. Buy one get two free, still no purchases. In fact, because of low demand, Mr Sugar decided to give away ten thousand Cubes without charge.

At first it seemed coincidental that three kids had a similar reaction and symptoms to me. But then hospitals started documenting frequent cases of exploding children. Doctors up and down the country compared notes. The same swollen tongue and bulging neck. They began calling it "Blowfish Face". When running through the list of foods eaten one item stayed prevalent. "The Cube". An urgent message was sent for all Sugar Nation's product to be destroyed due to health concerns. Local radio and international news broadcasters chased the story like police dogs seeking a clue.

Anywhere we turned reporters followed, searching for comments from my dad. They'd camp out on our front lawn taking pictures, sickening vultures. For the next two weeks the story ran on loop. Prime Ministers dropped their condemnation of Sugar Nation. An enormous backfire ensued; hundreds of people protested outside Sugar Nation's headquarters in central London. Angry parents whose children suffered "Blowfish Face" turned up in force. Placards and posters suggested what Mr Sugar could do with his sweets. Morning till night they'd chant, rave and holler. By all accounts the protest displayed utter disappointment in Sugar Nation's behaviour, peacefully.

'Oh no, we won't go. We'll stay here for months, weeks and hours because Mr Sugar's sweets have soured.'

Crowds got bigger; thousands squatted outside the building. But suddenly, the protesters characteristics differed. A younger set of disgruntled people swept in wearing Halloween masks armed with megaphones.

'Mr Sugar is a twit, a horrible man and miserable git, so come out here and eat my . . .'

Curse words are unkind and inappropriate.

The unrest cranked up, and groans were heard echoing through suburban streets. Unresolved frustration only leads to one outcome, violence, which never solves anything at all.

'Since Mr Sugar won't come and address us like human beings, we'll go to see him,' shouted a fuming protester with his face painted like a tiger.

'Yeah,' replied the rowdy rebels.

They ripped out a signpost using a sledgehammer to smash the pavement. Then, holding it sideways, they proceeded to ram the glass door to the building lobby. The bulletproof glass remained resolute. Once things turned physical, local authorities took the opportunity to use tear gas, smoke bombs and water cannons. The cannons delivered twenty litres per second, blasting demonstrators along street corners and back alleys.

'Scramble!' the water-soaked bodies lumbered away from the scene.

Sugar Nation wouldn't be capable of shrugging off such devastating publicity. So, Mr Sugar knew drastic action was completely essential. The dreaded words of corporate downsizing breathed across corridors, sending shivers down staff members' backs like a stubborn draught.

Senior executives were axed, with middle managers going too. Junior sales reps, senior sales reps and accountants were all booted out on their backsides. Hell, nothing was out of bounds; tables, chairs, desks, hole punchers, pencils and pens, anything that had the Sugar Nation emblem was trashed.

Mr Sugar blazed around the office cubicles covered in a snakeskin jacket. He prowled like a beastly lion tearing into timid prey.

'You needn't come in tomorrow. As a matter of fact, I never want to see your faces again,' he raged, flipping over desks, spilling hot coffee on the newly unemployed wages department.

'But sir, I've been with you from day one. I'm godfather to your daughter. In many ways you owe me,' said his ultra-loyal vice president, gazing into Mr Sugar's mint-green eyes.

'It's true, you've been there through a ton of battles. However, you're only as good as your last hit. Because I look at you like family, I won't fire you.'

The V.P felt light and free; friendship had spared him.

'I'll give you the dignity of resigning,' explained Mr Sugar.

'What? Your kids call me uncle.'

'Don't let the door hit you on the way out.'

***

Factories in Dudley and Newcastle which produced masses of Sugar Nation's goods ceased operating, making six thousand staff redundant. By Thursday, the majority of the workforce had been laid off.

After my penultimate day at school, I saw a weird sight ambling up the driveway. There was a strange male figure advancing towards my house. He looked scruffy, top button undone, tie hung loose around his neck and a coat obscuring his face. He donned a giant cardboard box containing a world's greatest dad mug and a Ginseng plant. I guess Mr Sugar final cleaned house and my father took the news on his chin, back and legs.

'Dad, where's the car?'

'Not now, son,' he flustered.

'But aren't we going to my piano lesson?'

21

'In life, son, you can't get everything you want,' he spoke very faintly. I could see tears appearing in the corner of his eyes.

Seeing how emotional father had become made me uncertain about our present and future. That night I listened closely to my parents' raised voices.

'We have no option. I've been blacklisted. Mr Sugar blames me for the lousy sales of The Cube.'

'I refuse to leave; this is my beautiful home,' yelled mom.

'You'll learn to love the new house. The real estate agent says it's in an up and coming neighbourhood,' promoted dad.

'Up and coming! Please. You mean some vacant, crumbling, cheap and old piece of . . .'

Cursing is a sin.

'Winterberry Street is a fantastic little area and it's in throwing distance of Winterberry High.'

Winterberry Street? Never heard of the place, but it sounds totally revolting.

'Winterberry High,' shouted mom.

'Yeah, I can't afford term fees at private school.'

'You want him to go to a state school with the working-class kids?'

'What's wrong with that?'

Mother never replied. She stormed out the room furiously.

Friday should have been a day of celebration. Unfortunately, Friday the 13th will always be associated with pain. I woke to the pleasant surprise of mom and dad both sitting on the edge of my bed. Mom's big bottom crushed my feet; don't tell her I said that.

'My darling boy,' beamed mom; her eyes twinkled engagingly.

'Ready for the last day of primary, son?'

I quivered. Heading into the unknown can be daunting. 'Sure, eager to learn.'

'That's my boy,' winked dad.

'Timothy and I will enjoy secondary school.'

There was an abrupt silence. My parents didn't have the gall to explain our financial difficulties.

Dad stumbled into his words. But the basic gist of the story went as follows: Mr Sugar terminated his contract and repossessed his company car. Now he'd be selling the house and we'd be moving to Winterberry Street ASAP. This drama was unwanted. Then again, how bad could Winterberry Street be?

When it was all said and done Sugar Nation was no more, forty years of sweet creations dismantled with one scandal. As for Mr Sugar, he turned his hand to a new venture. Well, sort of. He still sold sweets, only from a company called "The Nation of Sugar". Genius, where did he think of the name?

CHAPTER 4

Moving Day

Time had drawn to a close on my residency, and the old house felt deserted as we emptied it of our belongings. The walls were bare, without pictures of friends and family. Our sleek marble staircase now led to someone else's bedroom. The rare and unique Koi Carp that used to glide poetically around my pond now swam for a new owner's pleasure. The only thing I kept from my previous life was Einstein a stunning beagle and what's a man without his road dog. Mother kept the curtains closed for the longest period.

'If anybody asks why we're leaving, it's because we're moving to a bigger, posh and luxurious home.'

'Why don't you want them to know the truth?' I asked.

'They'll look down on us, casting judgement,' snarled mom.

'Don't yell at him, he's not to blame,' argued dad.

Mom shot him a vicious glance. 'Then who is at fault?'

'It's on me,' conceded dad. 'I can't find a job that'll pay enough to keep this house.'

My parents, on the surface, complemented one another like tea and crumpets. However, deep down, money ruled their relationship. And losing her five-star treatments put a strain on mom's happiness.

'A man of your calibre will soon rebuild, repair and achieve glory,' I rallied.

24

'Oscar, have one last look upstairs see if we've missed something,' said dad. My galvanising speech sparked no reaction; he kept his sorry, depressed state, dragging his feet.

I did the rounds upstairs, peering out of my former bedroom window. Suddenly I saw how the hierarchy of kid's friendships rapidly switch. Timothy had seized top spot. Victor slotted nicely into Timothy's old position, and Angus' stock rose exponentially from general outcast to third wheel. My three-year stint as head honcho had finished on a low note. Timothy's mom brought fresh sandwiches and lemonade up to his tree house. Their giggles sounded genuine, full of excitement. It was damning evidence to my already low self-confidence.

'Removal men will be here any second, son,' said dad, standing in the doorway.

'I should've told you about The Cube sooner.'

Dad placed his arms on my shoulders firmly. 'There's a reason behind everything; we just have to find it.'

'How can there be a good reason for this?'

'It's on you to make the best of a bad situation,' figured dad, rubbing my head. 'Do you want to go and say goodbye to your friends?'

The laughter radiating out the tree house sliced like a paper cut. 'What friends?'

'Don't talk soft, lad. Timothy is gonna miss you rotten.'

'Really?'

'Go on, you've got five minutes. You'll only regret it later,' implied dad.

Over the course of time Timothy had become my brother, a bond that'll never be broken. We were so close his mother at times had mistaken me for him.

'Oscar, hello, sorry to hear you're leaving,' she said, looking immaculate. Her skin was free of crinkles or wrinkles when she smiled. She wouldn't be seen dead without a summery dress on and earrings.

'Father's got a new job and needed additional space.'

She stopped ironing and pinpointed the weak story I'd given her. 'So, are six bedrooms and four bathrooms just not adequate for a family of three?'

'Sadly not.'

She sensed if she persisted, I'd fold. 'What sort of job is it?'

'Well, I'm not at liberty to discuss it. My father said it's classified information.'

Her probing halted. 'Timothy's in his tree house, go on up.'

'Thank you,' I had evaded her interrogation quite brilliantly, but Timothy's enthusiasm might pose stiffer opposition.

As I approached the trunk of the tree, even the bark was silky smooth. I crept up the ladder that had been carved into the wood. Timothy entertained his guests by doing a few impressions.

'Who am I? Father makes sweets. I get my way all the time. I'm loaded, rich and pick friends based on what I can take off them,' said Timothy, pulling off my accent.

'You're too funny,' giggled Angus.

'Spitting image, do his walk too.'

Timothy got me down to a tee. So much for buddy love.

26

Ah, forget Timmy, Victor and Angus; they'll be nothing without my abilities. I was the guy that cemented their status.

'Three cheers for Oscar the dictator,' announced Victor.

'Hip-hip-hooray,' declared Timothy and Angus.

I hung my head in humiliation and drifted home. The three amigos had made their opinions perfectly clear.

Anything and everything was bubble wrapped, boxed and labelled. Our most valuable possessions were double bubble wrapped then buried in Styrofoam. The finest china, silver cutlery and mom's beloved Victorian clock given to her by her great grandmother had special caution tape applied. Moving house is a mammoth task, a lifetime of moments compiled into boxes. The whole scenario felt tragic. Mom wore black, I wore black and father too; we were all in mourning. The end was nigh. A massive red removal van juddered up our drive.

'They're here. Let's get rolling people,' drilled dad.

This fat, lumpy man wearing a beige Removal & Approval uniform rattled the door knocker so empathetically it snapped.

'Hello, my good sir,' greeted dad.

'Nice to meet you mate. Sorry about the door knocker, don't realise my own power. Anyway, some other bloke's problem now,' said the grubby looking worker, dropping the metal knocker into dad's palm.

'I'd like you to start with the living room. Sofas first; if we get all the large items out first then our second trip will be a cake walk,' organised dad.

The removal man's head burst with delight; his head spun absorbing the wonderful décor. 'You were minted! Hand-finished floors and look at that fireplace. Wow! Must have set you back a couple quid?'

To me the fireplace wasn't spectacular. Yeah, it was flown in from New Zealand and mounted into the wall with real flames and a stone base that not only transmitted heat but also a magical scent of roses.

'Can you grab the other end of the couch?' asked dad.

Baz, the removal guy's name according to his name tag, seemed not to be in a hurry. He relaxed on the couch to phone a colleague.

'Leon, me old dog, what you up to? I've got a sweet gig here boy, I tell ya, a mansion, gorgeous crib. They've gone bust; cash strapped, broke, barely got a penny to their name,' he kicked off his shoe, poisoning us with his awful rotten-smelling feet.

'Listen, I'm not paying for you to lay about,' shouted mom.

He ignored mother's fury, selecting to give her a finger, not *the* finger, although it was still extremely rude.

'Are you gonna let him get away with this attitude?' asked mom.

'What would like me to do?' whispered dad.

'Lee, come down, hell they've got a pond,' he blabbed.

'As I stated earlier, big items are priority.'

'Well pardon me, I've been doing a fantastic job for two weeks since losing my last job due to damage to company property,' blurted Baz, undoing his belt buckle and letting his beer belly spread.

'Fills me with assurances,' raged mom.

'They had it out for me from day one. You take one forklift into a main gas pipe; injure six staff members and they feel it's paramount to give me my marching orders. Utter cheek.'

'You were hard done by,' reasoned dad.

'Have I got a tale of injustice? It involves me, a gorilla, five zookeepers and a penknife.'

'Can you tell me as we load?' wondered father.

'No can do, your goods are far too heavy. You wouldn't want me to throw my back out. Leon will be here in a while.'

A while in tradesman terms is one hour fifty minutes. This is an example I always carry; if you pay for budget work expect budget results. "Removal & Approval" charged by the hour, so delays were frequent. Leon pressed the doorbell so often the circuit board fried.

'Removal and Approval, here today gone probably by tomorrow,' said Leon.

'Your colleague says we can get started upon your arrival.'

Leon's eyes shot around the hallway, dazzled like a pinball. 'Blimey! Good gumdrops! I say, Bazza, you weren't kidding about this gaff.'

'It's insane. The kitchen is bigger than my house.'

'You know how to pick them, Bazza. What's a place like this go for?' questioned Leon.

'I rather not say,' shied dad.

'Did you bring my sandwich, Leon?'

'Bacon, eggs, sausages and tomatoes, otherwise known as a best.' He threw the foil package to Barry, who shredded the foil.

'My man, you don't disappoint. Problemo, where's the hot sauce? Meals aren't the same without it.'

A strong silence loitered. Bazza gawked at the sandwich as if it was a foreign object.

'Had you going,' smirked Leon, tossing several sachets of hot sauce.

'Time to refuel,' Bazza grinned, pouring the fiery red sauce onto the bread. As he sunk into it the egg slithered out, descending towards the pale coloured stone floor tiles.

'Unfortunate not eggs-actly the right result.'

Both men gobbled down their lunch; it was like watching a pack of wild animals. My old man wouldn't take this lying down. He'd have demanded their cooperation. But not now; he stood frozen, resigned to their tomfoolery.

The two idiotic removal men inspected each room thoroughly; they were completely engrossed by the refrigerator dispensing ice.

'How long before you get bored of this?' asked Lee, putting his mouth under the machine.

The longer we lingered our hurt and sorrow increased. A house we grew to love was set to be deserted.

'I've got to hand over the keys in one hour.'

'Bags of time,' said Leon.

The men pulled their acts together, slinging boxes onto their shoulders.

'Careful, fragile is written on it for a reason,' said mom.

Leon shook the box frantically.

'Were you dropped on your head as a child?' fumed mother.

'Sorry ma'am, just checking the security of your product.'

Barry and Leon began loading; packages were thrown in any which way. They threw items from room to room, cramming the van to bursting point.

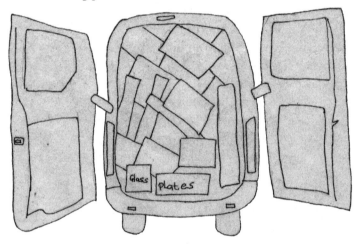

Only one possession remained; a huge, dark brown, leather couch. Removal was gonna be quite tricky.

'Remember lads, it's a corner sofa, so you want to tilt and spin.'

'Got you, my man,' nodded Barry.

The stupid removal men blew off dad's direction, slamming the sofa repeatedly and snapping the wooden door frame.

'Maybe we should tilt and spin,' said Barry.

'Fabulous idea,' praised Leon.

'I don't know where I come up with this stuff.'

Unimpressed, but hardly in a position to argue, we kissed goodbye to our old style of living rich for a much more low-key affair.

CHAPTER 5

Winterberry Road

The van bumbled and rumbled over the numerous ditches and awfully paved roads. Imagination is a powerful thing and in the wrong hands it will lead to disappointment. While awaiting my first glimpse of the house I'd be calling home, I gathered it would be reduced in size, probably four bedrooms, one and a half baths, detached and a two-car garage. Just basic really.

'We are getting closer,' said dad, faking a sense of excitement.

'Excellent,' a minute level of intrigue swept.

We ventured through narrow lanes and side streets. Addresses had weird names like Wolverine Place, Deadly Lane and Darkness Avenue. Derelict houses were pitched on rotting foundations; the ground crumbled and cracked underneath. The homes were so hollow you could see the backyard through the front. Children resembled refugees, their filthy torn clothes, unkempt hair and bare feet convincing me I was in for a rough ride.

'Look, there's some kids to play with. You'll make friends instantly,' said mom.

As I watched them roll around in the mud, I decided I'd stick to myself.

Reality struck me like a lead pipe, which was carried around like a fashion accessory in Winterberry Road. When slipping into the estate, a wall tagged with the greeting line "This is Winterberry Road enough siad". Pretty much summed up my next six months. By the way that's not a typo, they incorrectly spelt said. Grammar aside, the sky turned up bleak and bland clouds stalled over us. Winterberry consistently looked gloomy, as if it was neglected by the sun.

'You're in for a treat. They have laid on a welcoming party,' nodded Leon.

Leon drove deeper into Winterberry; neighbours stood on their porches eagerly eyeing up their new victims, or residents, depending on which way you analyse things. Our neighbours all owned tracksuits and smoked roll ups.

'You'll fit right in. Your fancy pancy designer brands won't be out of place,' laughed Barry, waving at the bystanders.

Mother was mortified; she grabbed a sunhat and sunglasses to conceal her face.

'We can't be rude to these people. They're a community,' explained dad.

'You forced us to move, but I don't have to engage with them,' cried mom.

'What happened to treat others how you want to be treated?' asked Barry, taking his eye off the road.

'Concentrate on the road,' barked mom.

'Crikey,' panicked Barry, curbing the front tyre then swerving to avoid the metal railings and the central reservation post.

'Too close for comfort,' sweated dad.

Barry decreased his speed. 'Only just got my license back. You do 80mph in a school zone and all of a sudden you're a menace to society.'

'Another conspiracy against you,' said mom.

'Tell me about it! Forty-seven times they've had me on bogus charges.'

Barry's the sort of guy who'd never admit guilt. He'd sit there and blatantly deny any wrongdoing.

'Here we are, number twenty-four Winterberry Road,' Leon pulled up on a slight gradient.

My eyes stayed firmly shut; I was reluctant to see our beastly new gaff. Gosh, I'm even starting to talk like them. Is poorness infectious?

'What your opinion, Oscar? thumbs up or thumbs down?' asked dad.

'It's a tremendous home,' I replied.

Dad prised my arms off my face. 'Son, it'll help to look properly.'

There's a handful of sights you wish you could reverse, like sneezing then peering into your hand afterwards. Well I don't always have a tissue prepared. I swallowed my diminishing pride and daringly opened my eyes.

'Tiny bit of tender love and care she'll serve you well,' said Leon.

Now obviously expectations were low but Geez Louise. The brickwork must've been left in the hands of a toddler. Red bricks started halfway up; yellow took over slowly followed by a light grey, and cement overflowed in areas, but nearing the roof seemed non-apparent. Also, I could locate more slate tiles on the floor than on our rooftop.

'If we put some elbow grease in it'll work miracles,' prompted dad.

I hope by *elbow grease* he means *demolition men*.

'What give you that impression?' whined mother.

'Once you've graced the inside with your creative brilliance, we won't notice a difference.'

Dad's deluded smiles were as transparent as clingfilm.

'On a shoestring budget I can't.'

'Only temporary; a qualified man like me will gain employment in days,' responded dad.

'We're up a creek without a paddle. I'm not certain we have a boat,' gassed mom.

'People come back from bad circumstances all the time. Yes, I'm down on luck, but still fighting.'

Father was attempting to use positivity to combat mother's negative spells. You know, always look on the bright side, because many people have it a lot worse.

Barry and Leon sat on the shoddy wall.

'Rich people slum it for five seconds and all of sudden it's a travesty,' said an annoyed Barry.

'Forget about that, Barry. If I'm to have a three-hour sleep before clocking out we need to hurry,' yawned Leon.

'Lady, gentleman and young one, sorry to be a bother we'd like to begin unloading please.' Barry spoke in the Queen's most perfect English.

Dad scrambled around in his pockets, seeking the key. It was an old type key; they're called skeletons. The long silver stem represented the body, for a skull the circular bow, and the bit that enters a lock also make up feet. He unlocked the door, pushing it with force.

'Looks to be jammed,' dad explained.

'Needs a real man's strength, no offence,' bragged Barry.

'Go for it,' said dad, stepping back.

Barry grunted, groaned, sighed and moaned, shoulder barging the weathered wooden door.

'Definitely stuck,' proclaimed Barry.

Leon wiped years of scum off the window glass using an ice scraper. 'Yeah, I can see the issue.'

The previous owners had wedged all their belongings against the front and back doors; mould and rust connected them together like a daisy chain.

'It just gets better and better. Can it get worse?' You did ask for it mom.

Dad's flustered body language inflated; he clenched his fist, tapping his head frequently.

'Stop beating yourself up. I got a crowbar; we'll snap the hinges,' offered Leon.

'Fantastic, we'll sleep with no door,' screamed mom. Her veins exploded.

'You haven't got a roof either. There's an unwritten rule about burglaries here; you wait two weeks before robbing newcomers blind. Or so they tell me,' said Leon.

'Get the tools, I'll call a locksmith,' conceded dad.

Leon walked back to his truck. A potent wind raged along Winterberry Road. I see where they get the name now.

'Is it me or is that truck moving?' I worried.

The van's wheels revolved, rolling backwards. Twenty-two Winterberry Road went by. Twenty Winterberry Road was blitzed by gathering speed.

'The parking brake! The parking brake!' bellowed Leon, chasing his haulage van down the street.

Kids on scooters and bikes jumped for dear life. The van surged on, wheels building energy, flattening a *no ball games* sign. Luckily, the road curved so the "Removal & Approval" van barrelled into a block of high-rise flats.

Blam!

With the impetus mustered it smashed through an entire wall as a family of fifteen ate beans on toast for tea, watching telly.

In fact, the family wasn't disturbed by the collision; they continued arguing about whose turn it was to do the washing up.

Leon put his hand up apologetically.

'Leon, you dozy Pollock,' vented Barry, slapping his colleague on the bonce.

'The cable must've sheared off. I hope you're able to accept my upmost sympathy,' begged Leon, addressing my father.

Every resident vacated the flat, staring at the truck shell-shocked.

'What happened?' speculated the neighbours.

'New family forgot to apply the handbrake.'

'Silly buggers,' said another neighbour, closing in on the crash site.

Twenty or so kids came and had a gander inside the truck. The adults supervised their meandering children, giving instructions.

'Look in the small boxes towards the back,' said one mother to her son.

Her little boy squeezed through the gap, opening our valuable items.

'Victory!' he threw out a diamond brooch.

His mother placed it in her palm; the carats shimmered as she moved her hand. 'It's real.'

'You better get down there,' told Barry, 'your authentic attire is living on borrowed time.'

We burst into a fast walk, Leon and Barry stayed a few steps behind in case the situation became violent. The van was vibrating; shaking, rocking and bopping it reminded me of one those American low riders. Families offloaded boxes frantically; they put Barry and Leon to shame. Our goods were launched around like a sick game of pass the parcel.

'See the way they're coordinated,' admired Barry.

'Highly functional teamwork can't substitute it,' replied Leon.

Now we were only a few paces away, a lookout whistled and, within a second the organised unit scattered.

'Let's take a peek at the wreckage,' said Barry, yanking the handbrake until it stopped clicking.

All five of us stared into the empty van.

'At least you don't have to worry about unloading,' Leon slammed the double doors shut.

'Our life is over,' wailed mother.

Dad attempted to pick up the pieces, salvaging the items dotted across the street.

Very stealthily Barry and Leon had crept into their van.

'You and I both know somehow we're gonna be made culprits, Barry.'

'Well let's skedaddle then.'

'We need Mr Smart to fill out a customer satisfaction form,' implied Leon.

'Why didn't you say?'

Barry wrote down a few raving comments about his service.

'Staff members were punctual, polite and a credit to your company. Signed Mr Smart,' Barry forged the signature.

The diesel-powered engine stuttered into gear and trickled off the pavement before belting down Winterberry Road.

'Oi, where you off to?' yelled dad; anguish lay in his voice.

'Take care, our job here is complete,' waved Barry.

Later that month Removal & Approval received thirty-one thousand client complaints. Big shocker.

CHAPTER 6

Yard Sale

On some occasions the best thing to do is to sleep on it. When we're asleep we're all equal: rich, poor, old, young, ill and healthy. I had a glorious snooze. I dreamt I never set foot in Winterberry Road. Unfortunately, due to the lack of slates, I could see the night sky; it brought true the definition of sleeping under the stars. Our mattresses were the only objects not stolen, aren't they thoughtful? The bedrooms weren't big enough to swing a baby mouse in; I could touch both walls with my hands.

Winterberry Road felt a world apart from my classy way of life. In theory it's a twenty-mile drive from my heavenly ex-home to the hell that is Winterberry Road. Cars, motorbikes drove strangely, their exhausts rattled, scraping speed humps, and people weirdly spoke to one another in a loud and brash demeanour. They'd grab each other in headlocks while constantly spitting, ghastly creatures. Odd pieces of metal were thrown on front gardens like decorations: old pipes, washing machines, kettles, bike frames and gas cookers. This confused the life out of me, then a lairy droning of a horn playing a tune that'd soon become familiar hit the street.

'Scrap iron! Any scrap iron! Scrap iron!' rung out from a speakerphone.

The truck whizzed along, carting off with every last bit of metal on offer. Dad flagged him down and the man was more than happy to haul away our tons of clutter. With the house gutted of rubbish we'd get a closer inspection of what lived beneath.

'Living room is quite spacious,' said dad, surprised.

Focusing on the flea-ridden carpet I noticed some suspicious looking yellow stains; a strong pong erupted now nothing was masking it. What a gross stench! I could taste it when I breathed, phew!

'Good solid walls, sturdy structures.'

Who's he kidding? Damp left black marks up and down the walls, corrupting the paint job. Add in the loose bricks and a peeling ceiling and dad had picked a winner.

'What about the green stuff growing out of the black fungus?' I questioned.

'A spring clean, lick of paint and it'll be a castle before you know it,' he replied, brushing a few bugs under the carpet.

'Stop the nonsense, it needs fumigating. A professional detox, then a builder to replace the horrendous brickwork and plastering on top.'

Mother may have come across as blunt, but father was delusional and believe me it's no good papering over old cracks. Deal with any issue head on. Not actually with your head, could be dangerous, I mean using common sense.

'Yeah, I'll get right on it,' contemplated dad.

'What are you saying?'

'D.I.Y. Grab a toolbox, Oscar and I will do the bits and bobs necessary.'

Dad wasn't a macho man, full of spit and grizzle. He'd rather a white wine than a lager, opera over sports and fashion over motors, but there's nothing wrong with that. So, D.I.Y sounded insane to me and I'm his most adoring fan.

'Think I'll have to pass.'

'Don't let your old man roll solo. We'll slide some of that grey thick mixture into the gaps and use a shiny flat instrument to smother the walls with plaster.'

He's referring to cement and the flat instrument is a trowel, for whoever was wondering.

'We need experts, real professionals,' demanded mom.

'Professional, you're just buying a name,' ignored dad, measuring the wall with his arms stretched.

'Ridiculous, I can't bear to be in the same room as you right now,' said mom, barging out of the front door.

'What's her problem?' shrugged dad.

Winterberry Road appeared busier than usual. Clusters of people walked, waltzed and plodded. Adults pushing kids in strollers on a family outing came from the left of me, rambling teenagers launching off ramps in shopping carts to the right of us.

'What a peculiar series of events,' I frowned.

'Must be a neighbourhood party. Grab your coat, Oscar.'

'Dad, we shouldn't mix with that bunch of repulsive idiots.'

There was a stern look in his eyes; he disapproved of my assessment. 'You're being rude. I taught you better than that.'

'They all stole our possessions, now you want to make nice,' I argued.

'Yes. The last thing we need is an estate hating us or we'll never get any peace.'

What happened to dad? He's surely an imposter. A mild-mannered parent taking everything in his stride will be eaten alive. To save dad's remaining dignity I did as told, grabbing my coat to see what Winterberry Road had to offer.

The road thrived, a whole gang of citizens standing in the middle of the street. Traffic was diverted. Why were grown men and women acting like barbaric vultures?

'Whatever you desire we cater to all needs: designer handbags, exotic perfumes and elegant footwear,' shouted an operator.

'I like that jacket,' enquired a customer.

'It's yours, fella. I have glamorous couture, clothes and accessories galore. How about a backless dress, stylish and finesse? An expensive men's suit, so you'll look cute. And for the little ones a remote robot, so purchase today only, cause that's your lot.'

Dad chiselled his way to the front, cutting in between the roaring crowd.

'I don't pegging believe it,' moaned father.

'Our prices are set for sale,' a dodgy male or female – hard to tell these days – grinned.

'Those are my goods.'

'Impossible, sir. I'm a well-respected retailer,' he protested.

Customers gushed over my awesome gadgets. They bought my helicopter, game console, tablets and laptops. I felt naked from a technology standpoint. What would I do for entertainment? Read books. The last thing I had to my name was Jerry. Jerry my voice activated robot. He cost as much as a small tropical island, but money well spent. Robots like him are humanoids, walking and talking; his battery life lasted up to six weeks. Jerry could do it all, cook, clean, move objects and answer any questions. Over one million sensors controlled him, meaning he was alert twenty-four seven, three hundred and sixty-five days a year.

'Can I interest anyone in a brand spanking new robot?'

'Give us a demonstration,' hollered the engrossed spectators.

The "retailer," despite gaining a financial windfall, floundered around Jerry's white plastic frame.

'People are waiting. Not a good look,' said dad.

'Stand back, my robot is preparing to amaze and dazzle,' he bragged.

The thief fondled every button on Jerry's back. Puzzled, he scratched his midriff.

'In a spot of bother?'

'Not at all, just reawakening the transmission. When stored in boxes the batteries go flat to reserve energy. A fantastic gadget and eco-friendly, last in stock, can't predict where I'll get another,' he persistently danced, waved, frowned and flapped, yet Jerry maintained his stance.

Father loved seeing this brash geezer get his comeuppance. 'Selling duds, are we?'

'I'm legit as they come. Ask anybody, my word is gospel.'

'Show me some legal documents of where you attained such items.'

The man stared at father clueless. 'Ah!'

'A receipt, all transactions come with an invoice.'

'I know your kind, con artist. Fake a posh accent, wear deodorant and convince innocent men you're righteous. Now, if you're not gonna buy anything, please move along.'

'Let's see what the police have to say.'

'Coppers, bacon, the pigs . . . no one likes a grass.'

'I couldn't care less how you rotten, trampy fleabags feel towards law enforcement,' jumped in mom.

Attention flipped simultaneously once the police were mentioned. They banded together; kind of nice how hatred kept the community tight.

'Don't do something you'll regret, mate,' pleaded the man.

Dad dialled digit 9. The neighbours gasped.

'Oh, sir, let's compromise,' he grunted.

Father proceeded to press a further 9.

'Bobbies only stick their fat noses in. They'll do massive damage to our lovely residence. You guys should be helping me too, all the dodgy equipment that resides in your homes.'

The crowd chipped in, aggressively backing father up. As dad's finger approached the final 9, a gang of five males rugby tackled him to the ground.

'You're causing me bodily harm, now release me,' whined dad while being restrained.

'Police are as popular around this neck of the woods as a debt collector. Ensure me you won't phone any authorities while living in Winterberry Road,' ripped the man.

Father struggled, wrestling, but the men kept him pinned down, applying more pressure.

'I need confirmation before we'll ease up.'

'No way Jose. My husband won't break, budge, bend or fold.'

Dad squealed like a baby pig.

'Won't he now?' said the fearsome man, loving a challenge.

'You can't intimidate us,' mom fired back.

'Stop antagonising them. We've just got off on the wrong foot, is all,' cried dad.

'Think a lesson in Winterberry Road's code of conduct is required,' revealed the man.

Gleeful decaying grins shot widely across their faces. Father lived in a high-intensity world managing multi-million-pound agreements regularly. However, Winterberry Road rattled his cage and danger stalked him continually. Whether it's a shambolic house, inadequate workers or six vicious thugs knocking seven bells out of him, dad urgently needed a resolution.

'I get the duct-tape. You find a safe location to perform the deeds,' winked the grimy man.

Four of the five men grabbed father by his arms and legs securely. The last gentlemen – and I use that term mildly – went off to probably steal supplies.

'Hey guys, I'm willing to reason,' father frowned while being led away.

The main man sniggered. 'Oh, now he wants a parley. You should have thought of that earlier. Sadly, Winterberry Road's rituals are sacred.'

They marched fifteen to twenty yards away from the yard sale. His yelling was swamped by the excited raving of the trailing residents. A good son rescues his papa, but the numbers game would prove too strong, for a human anyhow.

'Jerry, activate,' I ordered.

Jerry's electric face illuminated. His black visor projected "Welcome back Oscar, we've missed you." Glad someone does.

'Identify new humans.'

Jerry swivelled; in half a second, he scanned the motley bunch abducting dad.

'FOREIGN HUMANS AQUIRED. DISTANCE, FORTY- TWO POINT ONE METRES, ARRIVAL TIME APPROXIMATELY THREE POINT SIX SECONDS,' spoke Jerry.

'Deploy nutcracker.' Jerry boasted a dozen separate tools, sharpening, screwing, opening and cracking nuts, usually walnuts and almonds. Today Jerry is gonna have fun because Winterberry is littered with nutcases.

'INSTALLING NUTCRACKING SYSTEM, INSTALLATION SUCCESSFUL, PLEASE INSERT NUTS.'

'Jerry, use explore mode.'

'EXPLORING MODE ACHIEVED.'

'Explore!'

Jerry's rubber tracks rolled over the tarmac, zipping towards dad's kidnappers. His tracks were comfortable on any surface, and Jerry's speed was limited to 30mph. He flew down Winterberry Road with his metal pincer swinging left and right. On reaching the rowdy crew Jerry pinched, squeezed and prodded anybody and everybody. Ankles, knees, arms, toes and cheeks (and not the ones on your face) were twisted to within an inch of their lives.

Jerry's heroics had evened the playing field; dad was set free. Possession-wise we regained half our worldly treasures.

CHAPTER 7

Winterberry High

So, it's early September and we all know what that means, back to school. After six weeks of playing video games, watching movies and chillaxing returning to school can feel like picking at an old scab. But I was beginning a new era. Diamond Division hit my rear-view mirror; bring on secondary education. Life's full of transitions and no more so than the giant leap from primary to secondary school. Roles are reversed over the course of year 6 to year 7; children that were once big fish in small ponds now become tiny goldfish in an ocean.

There was a nervousness about me that sinister Monday morning. It took numerous tries to tie my shoelaces. I brushed my teeth half a dozen times, don't ask me why. My jitters weren't soothed by mother's calm exterior because she was head over heels with worry.

'Oscar, keep silent, these rapscallions won't take much of an invitation,' she panicked.

'Quit fussing, you're escalating the situation. All he has to do is not embarrass anyone,' said dad.

'What do you mean, father?'

'Son, I love you, that goes without saying. However, on a few occasions you correct people for speaking inaccurately. Doesn't bode good.'

'Doesn't bode well, dad,' I corrected him, cementing his theory.

'Right there. That'll kick you in the backside,' he confirmed.

Mother kissed me, slipping a five-pound note into my pocket. I knew we were struggling. Dad's search for employment continued three months since his eventful sacking from Sugar Nation. He and mother spoke frequently of the currently weak climate, but the weather seemed OK to me.

'Mom, I don't need additional cash,' I left the note on the coffee table.

'Honey, every penny is vital,' confessed dad.

'Those school bullies, seeing my darling boy so handsome, will bombard him and take his lunch money.'

Do bullies still take lunch money? Well, I guess it's a prosperous business.

'Would you like me to walk with you?'

Now, I'm trying to evade bullies, not accept them with open arms. So, turning up to school hand in hand with mommy would only add fuel to a pretty stocked fire.

'No thanks,' I replied politely.

'Come straight home, understand?' she kissed me again; her red lipstick marked my forehead. 'My little man all grown up.'

'Bye, mother.'

'Wait, where is my camera?'

'Oh man. Do you have to?'

'Yes, big school is a momentous jump,' she snapped a pic head on. 'Great, turn to your left please.'

'What?'

'I want pictures from all angles.'

'But why?' I asked.

Mother came closer; she bent over slightly, whispering softly. 'In case they need an up-to-date photo for the milk carton.'

'Give over, he'll be fine. State school isn't half as bad as it's professed to be.'

'How would you know?' said mom.

Dad's quietness displayed an inability to give evidence. 'Focus and show no fear.' Dad shook my hand, sending me off.

Winterberry High, where do I start? Now going on the assumption it was constructed by the cowboys who built Winterberry Road, the school could only be a disaster zone and delivered in a fitting way. Initially windows had been smashed so many times they were replaced by bricks, and the stairs leading to the main block were crooked and significantly missing chunks of concrete. On a huge tower rested a clock, keeping time with Roman numerals. Work this out – I've been here for ten minutes from eight thirty, yet the old, rusty clock said ten past nine.

I waited outside the structure, petrified my parents had tainted my mind.

The school bell rung sharp and loud.

Two overloaded double-decker buses charged up to the collapsed gates. Kids budged together standing, sitting on each other's laps; a few even hung out the doors. Hundreds of rough and tough teenagers flooded the school grounds. Tall, burly lads rushed off

48

the buses, their clothes stretched and war-torn. In fact, a few boys owned mutton chop sideburns, lucky buggers. I gazed at their grumpy faces as they offloaded.

One kid in particular took a dislike to my observing. He marched over assertively.

'Oi, what you looking at?'

'Nothing at all,' I smiled.

'You calling me nothing?' he growled in a deeper voice than mine.

'No, I wasn't looking.'

'Am I lying? You were eyeballing me from the get go. Do we have beef here?'

'Beef? No beef. I like turkey myself,' I responded.

'You've got some cheek, lad, for a year 7.'

Before this boiled down to a fistfight, which I could have taken, a school teacher appeared and saved his bacon.

'Morrison, what are you doing?'

Morrison gently patted my shoulder. 'Helping the new guy find his feet. Now all first day students arrive in the assembly hall for introduction.'

'You are a good kid, Morrison. Despite your past aggression problems,' praised the teacher.

Morrison signalled with his thumb up. 'I try, sir.'

Most year 7s retreated into the assembly hall for our welcoming pack. We were like sitting ducks; any one of us could be abducted. When out in the wild, less ferocious animals travel in packs. I'd need to find a team to survive. Children that are more unpopular and less intelligent, so I'd get a break. Hey, I don't make the rules.

Morrison stomped to his class. Dodged a bullet there, Oscar. And breathe. I gallantly strode towards the assembly hall two minutes late. There the head of our year, Mr Trent, unfolded how our school term would break down. Mr Trent used my lateness as an example to all.

'Always one child who feels he is above the rest,' he snarled.

'Sorry sir, I was in an altercation with another student.'

'Troublemaker. Brawling on my premises is total forbidden. I have my eye on you.'

'But he instigated it.'

Mr Trent placed me in front of my classmates. 'Children like him are the horrible brats we won't appreciate. They'll disrupt classes, always have an excuse available and ruin the learning experience for others.'

'I'm nothing of the sort,' I said, defending myself.

'You're pushing your luck, son. No more lip. Now find a seat, preferably near to me,' he shouted.

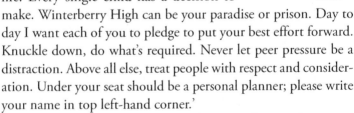

Mr Trent was a youngish teacher, maybe mid-twenties, unfortunately dressed as though he'd been defrosted. Seriously, who wears braces instead of a belt, along with a pair of tanned boat shoes? But the most horrific sight was his awful comb over. If a hairline starts at the back of your head, best bet is to let it go. Honestly, if time machines are ever invented send him back to 1830. Although the room had two hundred and fifty new and eager children, Mr Trent directly aimed his speech at me. He'd point, stare and hover by my chair.

'Today is the first day of the rest of your life. Every single child has a decision to make. Winterberry High can be your paradise or prison. Day to day I want each of you to pledge to put your best effort forward. Knuckle down, do what's required. Never let peer pressure be a distraction. Above all else, treat people with respect and consideration. Under your seat should be a personal planner; please write your name in top left-hand corner.'

Two hundred and forty-nine students simultaneously put pen to paper. All except one; when I scrambled about under the chair all I retrieved were crumbs, dust and bellybutton fluff.

'Are you all up to speed?' he asked.

Yes sir,' repeated the classmates together.

Mr Trent breezed by my energetic motioning.

'On the next line I request your guardian's name and home address.'

Again, desperate children keen to impress scribbled down more information.

'Here comes the fun part, on the back page is your timetable. These are your lesson guides with classrooms also stated.'

I waved both arms furiously, as if I was landing an aircraft. He's blanking me on purpose.

'Make your stay here a joyful and wonderful experience,' Mr Trent smiled.

'Sir,' I shouted; the volume boomed off the ceiling.

Mr Trent stopped his conversation dead. He swiftly turned into my space and raced over so we were face to face. His bulbous nose pressed against mine.

Two hundred and forty-nine kids cringed, flabbergasted, expecting me to get read the riot act.

'Where are your manners? Hands up when asking a question, little squirt. You're not special; probably fancy yourself as a big man on campus. Wait until you're spotted rather than barging in. Got it?'

'I'm extremely sorry, sir. But I haven't received my planner.'

Mr Trent backed off, huddling with his teachers and chatting about this predicament. Due to my late registration Oscar Smart didn't figure on their system. If Winterberry High wanted to pretend I never existed then fine, because the feeling's mutual. Everything I got from there on was makeshift. They told me to follow Lance. Lance looked a humble, down-to-earth person who I could see myself being friends with.

By the closing of induction day, Winterberry High had already had a profound effect on my character.

CHAPTER 8

Four Wheels

After an awful number of downfalls, rejection and tremendous misfortune, father was hired by a company called Parcel Express as a night manager. Obviously, the bravado and glamour of Sugar Nation couldn't be duplicated. He also took a hefty pay cut. In actual fact, seeing my father a working man out of his mini funk was worth its weight in gold.

By Saturday dad had got his groove back and only felt it appropriate to get himself a new ride. While employed by Mr Sugar he received a car allowance, giving him free rein over a handful of elite motor vehicles. I'd usually try to goad him into the supercharged V8 expensive saloon cars. Only dad was always concerned about fuel consumption. Cool and replenishing juices were amply served by staff. The who's who of modern engineering sold their best automobiles from here. Stylish Italians, well-equipped Germans and intelligent Japanese manufactures held premiere places in the window. I shouldn't harp on the past; it stirs up too many painful emotions. I'll never forget the car dealer at the showroom; we had a running joke.

'Which one is it today, sport?' he asked.

'Surprise me,' I'd reply.

He'd toss me a pair of keys to the latest sports model.

'Fire her up, give it a tickle.'

Motors this exclusive don't start the way you'd automatically think. No keys. So I slipped a card into the main dashboard reader and then slammed the "engine on" button. A spine shattering tremor pulsed out, the monstrous noise exaggerated in the closed off showroom.

'Let's hit the highway, son. Belt on and flick the lever behind your right hand.'

That's another thing about these extravagant machines; they no longer had stick gearboxes, instead opting for flappy paddle ones on either side of the steering wheel.

'My feet can't touch the pedals.'

However, year to year as I grew, that accelerator pedal became ever more visible.

'Oh well boy, not today.'

'Gosh darn it,' I'd complain.

Then he'd eject the key card and would leave me with a word of encouragement in my ear. 'Oscar, if you study super hard, stay determined, committed and honest you'll have a car collection of your very own.'

'Do you really think so?'

'I promise. Follow in your father's footsteps and impossible is simple. Provided you buy the cars from me mind. Someone's gotta get paid, why not me?'

We chuckled while dad analysed the miles per gallon on another boring saloon.

Unfortunately, the sequence was now yesterday's news. But who knows what's around the corner?

It's not out of the realm that the auto dealers at "Bargain Cars & Bikes" will also be heart-warming, friendly and productive. Deleting the last sentence doesn't do "Bargain Cars & Bikes" justice. I'm not entirely positive if we were entering a thriving car business or a local scrapyard. Columns of battered second, third, fourth and fifth hand heaps of junk had their bonnets open with mechanics spinning spanners and twisting wrenches steadily. Engine parts vaulted into the sky; it was raining nuts and bolts.

'Watch out for the oil slick, Oscar,' instructed dad.

'Yikes dad, can't we go back to our original dealership?'

'Not at the moment son, see we're looking for a comfortable runner reasonably priced.'

Father skipped around the disc brakes, mufflers and piston rings reaching the building.

'Welcome, welcome,' said the dealer, seeming grungy in appearance. Used car dealers have a shiftiness about them, constantly moving and gabbing away. 'You want vehicles? You've come to the right place. Up top, little squirt.'

I slapped his slippery palm; it felt like plunging my hand in petroleum jelly. Thankfully I carry hand sanitizers everywhere.

'Yes, I wish to purchase a vehicle of sound body and engine for a relatively good fee,' said dad.

'Seek and you shall find. Look no further; feast your eyes on our wonderful yet unique range of vehicles,' snapped the wheeler dealer.

'I'm in the hunt for a run around – nothing too pricey, we're on a tight budget.'

'In that case come along,' the dealer shuttled to the back entrance. 'This is what we call bargain basement, low cost and no fuss.' He put his arm out far and wide as if unveiling something special.

At the back of the car lot a world of unusual and rare motors were harboured. Vehicles from decades previous like Morris Minor, Austin Healy and Ford Capri were listed. Bring a hundred quid with you I'm confident you'd drive or push away a fleet of automobiles and have change to spare.

'I thought you were going to buy a car for the road, not banger racing,' I said.

'Don't be so crude, Oscar,' shouted father.

'But that car is sitting on house bricks! Others have flat tyres and this one is missing an engine,' I explained.

'I never stated we sold exquisite transportation. Bargain Cars & Bikes offer spectacular value for money.'

Dad gazed at each deadly vehicle thoroughly before performing the very mannish duty of kicking the tyres and pulling out the dipstick.

'Sir, stop mooching around, my equipment is examined by trained and skilled guys,' panicked the wheeler dealer.

He stumbled over with his grizzly black hair melting into chest. He was so hairy it came across as though he wore a black woolly jumper underneath his Hawaiian shirt, with five gold medallions suffocating in the darkness.

'Buddy, I never trust word of mouth,' said dad.

'As you were,' the dealer frowned.

Father held the dipstick upside down; its metal gauge was as dry as an African desert in summertime.

'Dipstick is in superb shape,' implied dad.

The car dealer pointed his finger in a jubilant manner. 'There's a man who knows about internal combustion engines.'

'I'm familiar with the engine.'

'Boy does it show. Why didn't you say? I got a car for you as good as new.'

Behind the cluster of rust buckets lay a bright orange saloon, tyres fully inflated, four doors and functioning headlights, shockingly.

'If you search long and hard enough, you'll be rewarded with a gem,' noted the wheeler dealer as he opened the driver's side door.

'Colour is a bit flash,' said dad, unsure.

'Cars are to be seen, not heard. Tell you what, take her for a test drive then come to a conclusion.'

I rode in the back seat after the dealer claimed shotgun. Dad strolled off the lot, snaking past the mounting pieces of car items balancing in a leaning tower.

'Nothing more magnificent than an open road,' beamed Mr Wheeler. 'Cruising down the highway is so relaxing.'

The car jerked and jolted away none too convincingly.

'Sturdy performer, only one lady owner and just twenty-six thousand miles on the clock. For its age that's marvellous,' he declared.

'Steering wheel is pretty smooth, turns right and left quite precise,' said dad.

'Where's the radio?' I wondered.

'There it is, young fella,' said Mr Dealer, tapping this enormous wooden box in the centre console.

'Where?'

'It's concealed. Prepare to be amazed.'

He slid up the wooden panel which contained this rather peculiar rectangular silver box.

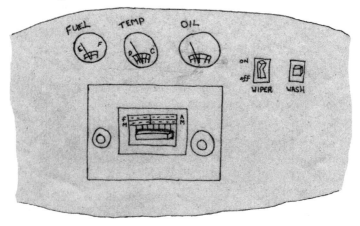

'What the heck is that?'

'An eight-track tape player, son. Back in the day before mp3s, USB and even CDs, eight-track tapes were the best and only way of listening to portable music.'

He spoke as he shoved a bulky cartridge into the massive slot. About a minute later the tunes spluttered out of three of the four speakers. The quality wasn't as pure as new age systems, but the beats sounded neat and nifty.

'How does it work?' I questioned curiously.

It was a question he itched to answer; anything to distract dad from the clunking engine noise.

'Well, eight-track tape players originated in America. Since 1964 it became a raging success and long tedious drives were soon forgotten. Inside the cartridges lives a thin film reel, which is held on a loop; when selected to play, the tape is pulled up towards the main playback head, where the information is pinched off the film and projected for our enjoyment.'

Usually not my cup of tea, but Mr Wheeler made some out-of-date technology appear somewhat riveting. I had a multitude of follow-up questions to ask.

'So how did we get from tapes to where we are now?'

Mr Wheeler spun his head round rapidly; his eyes glowed, excited by my enthusiasm.

'Love people that are probing for historical facts.' He patted my knee gently.

'History is the most knowledge you'll ever receive. To know our direction, we must learn from others who paved the way.'

Mr Wheeler preached the truth; history is ultra-important. It's here to explain old systems so we can improve the future.

'Hope you're listening, Oscar,' added dad, heading into a tunnel.

The tunnel was dreadfully lit, long and winding. Father switched on the full beams; its headlights stretched the length of the road. As we escaped the dark hole, Mr Wheeler continued to describe how we evolved from eight tracks to cassette Walkman then eventually to the mp3 and mp4 players we take for granted today.

'Where will they go next?'

'I predict they'll come up with a device that'll digitally download songs into your eardrums,' replied Mr Wheeler.

'Really?'

'Wouldn't put it past them, science is ever developing.'

The orange automobile had held its own. The only thing I realised was Mr Wheeler's actions; his feet were spread apart, avoiding the middle area of the foot well.

'Tax for six months and I'll throw in an MOT on the house.'

Dad remained calm, not giving away if Mr Wheeler's generosity was a major selling point.

'How good of you,' dad informed, sinking the clutch for third.

Whenever father went for a gearshift Mr Wheeler apparently suffered from a terrible cough. Second gear cough. Third gear loud cough. Four gear continuous cough. Fifth gear a damn near seizure.

'You satisfy a customer once, they'll always return,' said Mr Wheeler, firmly lodging his knee against the car door panel.

'Nippy vehicle, good interior, I'll have it.'

'Splendid, fantastic, brillo,' clapped Mr Wheeler. 'Back to the dealership we roam.'

Dad reversed into the car lot. Mechanics halted their work. Seeing Mr Wheeler's mucky mitt fixed on my dad's shoulder confirmed the sale. All the mechanics stood silent, coming up stumped.

'He's incredible. I'm sure he could charge people for using sand at a beach.'

'I don't know how he sleeps at night,' whispered the men.

Mr Wheeler brought out all the necessary legal paperwork. 'Let's get you going.'

Money changed hands and father now sadly, not proudly, owned an orange saloon which wasn't the full ticket. As dad signed and printed his name, Mr Wheeler hadn't entirely finished swindling away my father's resources.

'Are we up to scratch?' asked dad.

'Just as precaution, I'd like you take out the extended guarantee,' he offered.

'Why, do you expect me to have problems?'

'Absolutely not.'

'Then I'm not interested,' replied dad, heading for the door.

'However, say a freak hazard occurs, I won't be in a position to help,' smirked Mr Wheeler.

There was a polite silence, if silences can be polite. Both gentlemen saw and understood where each other was coming from. Who'd fold first?

'Just an extra hundred pound,' informed Mr Wheeler.

'I can live with that.'

'Outstanding. Since you're purchasing you might as well take up the option of a limited warranty.'

Wheeler dealing at its finest; they sell you a car originally. Then additional extras like limited warranty, payment protection, extended guarantee and deposit insurance. Within a tick you've bought a car for twice the price.

CHAPTER 9

Girls

Now Winterberry High had a lot of differences, the most glaring one being that of girls. Coming from an all-boys school to a mixed one would take some serious adjusting. Up until this point the only women I had known were mom, a few aunties, grandma and my friends' mothers. So, having girls my age around made a nice if not smooth change of pace. There comes a time in every young boy's life where girls stop being these yucky creatures and fill you with jitterbugs in their presence. Well, year 7 definitely signalled the switch; a few girls were on Oscar Smart's radar if I ever found the courage to speak to them.

Phoebe Smallwood I'd selected to be the first girl to see my charm. Her mousy brown hair dropped below her shoulders and she owned the most dazzling pair of sapphire blue eyes. In our art class, boys and girls had a seating plan alongside each other, in alphabetical order. Smallwood and Smart. See, it's fate. I pulled out her chair as gentlemen do. She did an eye roll and glanced at me pathetically.

'Hello, I'm Oscar Smart. It's a pleasure.'

'Don't talk to me. I wouldn't want to give the others the impression we're friends,' said her ice-cold face.

I think they call it playing hard to get.

Each art class had its own set theme. Horror was today's lesson, the task to draw something as gruesome, hideous and vulgar as humanly possible. What could I draw from for inspiration? Easy, the house I sparingly call a home.

'I want you to be experimental. Dabble with colour creations, take your mind and explore its darkest place,' said the teacher animatedly.

Art is one of those lessons – either you get it, or you just don't. I was for the latter. My scribbles came out like garbage; even as a wee child I couldn't stay inside the lines colouring.

'I'm sure your picture will result in perfection, Phoebe,' I said.

She placed her large canvas in front of my desk. 'What don't you get about not chatting?' she fumed.

'Just complimenting you on your project is all,' I said, outlining my house.

Looking back on my conversational skills I sounded desperate, weak and sad.

Phoebe took art way too serious. She pulled out a gigantic pencil case – it wasn't a pencil case you or I may carry with pens, pencils, rubber, ruler and protractor if you're posh. Hers consisted of glitter, glue, palette, acrylic and watercolour paints. She had a special unit for her glorious paintbrush set. Phoebe's brushes had plastic protecting their bristles. Inscribed on the black handles were numbers for a specific use: flat, round, bright, broad, stroke and glaze wash among others.

'Wow. You love your art.'

'Shut up,' she snapped back, looking at the shape of my head.

A few girls next to us began whispers about me.

'You think that's his girlfriend?'

Phoebe stood up and bellowed out the infamous words. 'Oscar Smart isn't a friend or acquaintance. He's a loser by all accounts and it hurts my eyes to look in his direction.'

The classroom of thirty clapped intensely, banging the windows and tapping their pencils against the table.

I'm kind of sensing she's not the one, all being said.

'Let your feelings be known,' I mumbled, mortified.

'Just nipping these rumours in the bud. I hate rumour mills,' she said, holding her thumb up to my face.

So, my first encounter with girls was a complete bust, but when you fall off the horse, you have to immediately get back on.

After Phoebe's outburst the class trailed off and students dedicated themselves to their pictures. Frantic hands streaked across papers and rubbers were in use, making subtle detail alterations. As for mine, the house started badly, remained atrocious and ended tragically.

'Way to go Phoebe, it's really taking shape,' said a few admirers.

'I feel my artistic nature whizzing into my veins,' Phoebe was being compelled by her canvas. She wedged a paintbrush in her teeth, staring at my skin complexion.

'What are you drawing?'

'You'll see soon enough,' she mixed two parts white to one part pink.

She left me intrigued. Every now and then she'd peer above her canvas, glance then add another splash of paint. Is it possible Phoebe made a rash decision?

'Right class, how are we progress-wise?' asked the teacher, wandering around the room.

One thing I've learnt today – Oscar Smart can cross animator, graphic designer, painter or any sort of craft profession off his career list.

The teacher breezed about the classroom and peeked at several pictures before setting her focus on Phoebe's piece.

'My motivation was unstoppable; it overpowered me, miss.'

The teacher's eye enlarged ecstatically. 'Everybody, pencil down and marvel at this young lady's sensational work. You don't move a muscle, Oscar.'

Twenty-eight students stepped towards Phoebe's canvas.

'You're fabulous. You must call it something; a creation so devious and sickening needs a name,' gushed the teacher.

Phoebe rubbed her cheek in contemplation then announced it to all, 'the haunted one.'

'Excellent, a fitting name for such a ghastly human being,' explained the teacher. 'Love how you got the distance between the forehead and his thick, bushy eyebrows correctly.'

Thick bushy eyebrows . . . I own a pair of bushy eyebrows.

'You got the arch in the nostrils sublimely.'

'Yes miss, as I look at his horrible face the right side is slightly deformed.' Phoebe pointed to my nose.

'What do you reckon, Oscar?' questioned the teacher, spinning the picture that had an uncanny resemblance to me.

'Not a huge admirer of cartoon characters,' I said, blushing.

'You have no value in art,' screamed the teacher. 'This one is going up, entitled "the haunted one."'

My classmates cackled, chanting "the haunted one". Their beady eyes revelled in enjoyment.

'The haunted one! The haunted one! The haunted one!'

I became freaked out; this class suddenly turned sinister and evil, holding the painting above their heads.

The school bell rang, ordering the conclusion of my most bizarre lesson thus far.

Winterberry High held only two after school activities, football or performing arts. Sliding about a field gaining stud marks and injuries wasn't appealing. Guess I'll have to venture into the unique world of acting.

Now, the performing arts department was run by a wonderful teacher called Miss Louise, who had a bubbly personality. Rehearsal took place in the main hall, and a big production was arranged for the end of term. I happened to be the only boy among a sea of girls from year 7 through to 11.

'Is this rehearsal?' I asked, quite nervous.

Miss Louise glowed, delighted to finally have a boy about. 'Ladies, welcome our first male performer.'

The girls neither blinked nor greeted me. Oh boy.

Their production of Romeo and Juliet, put simply, sucked eggs. I don't quite remember William Shakespeare's classic being so foul. There was no coordination; people strutted out on stage incapable of following directions. They missed words and cues and shunted each other during mid-sentence.

'That's my line, idiot,' blazed one girl, jumping up in another's face.

'Ladies, please,' said an anxious Miss Louise.

'Where the red markers are on the script is where I speak,' confirmed another girl.

'Aren't you Romeo?' asked girl one.

'I'm playing Mercutio.'

The original girl shuffled through pages, realising her hiccup. 'I'll let you off then.'

Miss Louise watched her drama dwindle into a slagging match, although the fight sequences were pretty realistic and grisly. But for every shoddy moment I endured, they were blasted away when the star attraction arrived, oh Juliet. Juliet, a.k.a Rachael Lily, a flower for a flower. She approached from stage right. The rag and bone girls were subdued, their envious faces transformed to stone. Her solo performance amazed me. Her voice spoke to my soul drawing me near.

'She's insightful and innocent,' I said, standing underneath the stage.

As she twirled and twisted a couple girls had seen enough, shoving her off stage. I ran. Rachael wobbled, teetering – it all played out in slow motion. I covered ground like a cheetah hunting a  gazelle. Rachael's scream emanated with elegance and grace. She fell head over heels into my arms.

Miss Louise was giddy; she flipped and flopped, enthralled. 'I see it. The emotion. You care for her. I feel that tingling spark. A romance. Ladies, our main stars for Romeo and Juliet are Oscar and Rachael.'

'You'll be seeing a lot of me,' I winked.

'She's drew the short straw,' giggled the ogres up on stage.

Rachael shrugged me off, disgusted even by the idea of us co-starring. 'Miss, I'd rather quit.'

'Why are you being so difficult? You're my superstar actress.' Miss Louise said.

'I refuse to work with such a revolting boy. He smells like he lives in a dumpster.'

Wow, a smaller person would take this to heart.

'Come on, it's named acting. Pretend he's someone else.'

'Professionals of my style won't be able to gloss over this torture,' she hissed.

Torture! OK, I'm officially hurt.

Miss Louise stood frustrated. 'Would any of you girls play Juliet?'

The girls' hand arced up as if they were attempting to touch the ceiling.

'Good. You do understand Oscar will play Romeo?'

Hands shot down back into their pockets. My luck with the ladies is remarkable. But, if you're initially unsuccessful, dust yourself off and pick yourself up again.

CHAPTER 10

Eye Eye

My Winterberry female ranking died a thousand deaths and showed no sign of a revival. I wisely decided to put my love life on hiatus. I lived for the weekends; at least there I was free and safe. Unfortunately, this weekend I had a special appointment with the opticians. Eye doctors are one of my pet peeves, along with normal doctors and dentists. They seem so scary in their white overcoats and rubber gloves asking delicate questions about personal issues. Mind your own business Nosy Parker.

Mother hadn't left her creature comfort lifestyle behind. She polished her best glad rags.

The optician stood by the door to the testing room. 'Mr Oscar Smart,' he summoned.

I need your opinion on something. Don't you find it astounding that all opticians wear glasses? Maybe if your vision is impaired then you shouldn't be allowed to test others.

The optician glanced at my mother's dolled up attire. 'Excuse me love, would you like to come along?'

'Pardon?' asked mom.

'Some kids feel more settled with a parent there to keep them calm,' explained the optician.

'Why do I need to keep calm? You're just doing a check-up, right?' I asked worried.

'See, he's riddled with fear. Mother, I'm gonna insist you join us,' smiled the optician.

'If it's what's best,' said mom, cupping my cheek.

The optician swiped a card across the glass panel. 'Oscar, prop yourself up on that chair.' He stopped mom by the door speaking softly. 'May I say you're as pretty as a button. How can he be your son? Was there a mix-up in the hospital? Or is he adopted?'

'Thank you, I'll tell my husband that one,' said mom, flashing her wedding ring.

'Husband,' he said, wildly disappointed.

'Yes, we're happily married,'

'Heard loud and clear, I'll be doing a very sincere and very thorough exam of your son's eyes.'

He pulled the string cord, killing the light. His devilish face reflected off the lit-up eye chart behind him.

'Let's get crack-a-lacking,' he nodded, rolling his chair over to my testing seat.

I so didn't require a pair of glasses; bullying at Winterberry High would surely reach epidemic level. My eyes had to play their role, stay focused and sharp.

'Right, first test. Follow my finger,' instructed the optician.

'Very well, sir.'

He began shifting his index finger left to right then up and down slowly. If this examination continues in this vein, I'll coast it. Suddenly, his finger zoomed left, up, down, right, up, up again, right, right, right some more, left, down and a further right up. I couldn't keep track of his movement.

'That's totally unfair. You can't expect him to maintain concentration with your finger going like the clappers,' defended mom.

The optician stopped his questionable exam. 'Who here has a qualification in eye stuff?' argued the man aggressively.

'Eye stuff?' said mom, miffed.

'Yes, I believe it's the correct term.' He shot a torch upon the wall towards a certificate.

Mom simmered down, still dissatisfied but unable to argue with his credentials, so allowed him to proceed.

'If you don't mind letting me do my job.'

My eyes were producing enormous amounts of water. I'm unsure if they were tears or watering from constant poking and prodding.

'Eye motion is stable,' he said.

Phew, at least my eye inspection was done with. As I gradually got up, happy to be exiting, he abruptly clicked a button that tilted the chair smacking my head against the headrest.

'I'm not finished just yet, Oscar,' he spoke menacingly.

What did I do in a past life to deserve this? I must have been an evil dictator.

His action became overwhelming; it went from a regular exam to formal operation. The man squeezed droplets of liquid into my pupils. It burned, hurt and now my eyes barely worked.

'Oscar, could you please read the chart?'

The chart remained six feet away; oddly enough the letters were written in symbols. He fitted me with some adjustable glasses, slotting a blank lens in front of the left eye, obstructing its view.

'That chart?' I said hesitantly.

'Just read as much as your eyes will permit,' explained the optician gently.

Here goes nothing.

'Squiggly line, 7, dot, Z, 5, hedgehog, star, arrow, four.'

'Interesting, Oscar, extremely impressive,' the optician chuckled. 'Let's test the left eye.'

At this stage the fluid inside my left eye funnelled out. I blinked furiously, trying to rid myself of the potent stinging.

'When you're ready,' he stated.

The chart looked vague; its black lettering and white background now swirled into grey.

'S, P, 1, 3, 3, turtle, hamster, caterpillar, women line dancing, two frogs kissing,' I said, freestyling.

'They're funny glasses you got from the joke shop,' slammed mother.

'Listen ma'am, my abilities are as sound as a pound, and I for one am getting pretty irritated by your two cents,' he moaned.

'It's not possible he can't read those words in bold letters.'

The optician smirked, bemused. He then flashed a powerful bulb deep into my eyeballs; the beam felt so dynamic I reckon the light shined through the back of my head. 'OK, I've seen enough from you.'

Finally, this optical exam straight out of the gates of hell ended.

'Indications reveal you're as blind as the blindest of bats. Surprised you haven't walked into stationary objects already lad. I prescribe glasses that should be worn at all times, including sleep,' documented the optician.

'Including sleep?'

'Definitely, little fella. Your eyes are so deteriorated even dreams will come out blurred.'

'I demand a retest. I've never had trouble with eyesight before.'

The optician bore down on me. From what I saw, his figure was faint and faded. 'Are you sure you'd want to repeat this again?'

The eyeball tingling stayed prevalent. It felt like a hundred ants racing towards the pupil. I weighed up my dreadful options: risk permanent injury by withstanding another exam or pick a pair of God-awful bifocals. What a real bummer.

'I'll wear the specs,' I conceded.

'Excellent,' he cheered.

I sagged a lot, as if all my bones had been ejected from my body.

'Hey, glasses help the near-sighted see far and the far-sighted see near.'

'Which one am I?'

'Oscar, you're in a unique category for the short, narrow, long, very long and blurred sighted. But there's tremendous news, my friend.'

'Nothing good can or will be achieved here.'

'Nonsense, every exam when a person is recommended glasses is free,' he said, putting his thumb up.

'Yippee,' I spluttered sarcastically.

'Sarcasm is not the answer,' said mom.

We left the examining room to find a suitable pair of eyewear.

Glasses can be a fashionable expense; however, Eye Eye's collection didn't take that into consideration. Their kids section consisted of a handful of pathetic, rigid and almost extinct frames. Chic, hip, trendy, swanky or stylish were never words uttered on Eye Eye's property.

'Spoilt for choice, aren't you, Oscar?'

'Is it that obvious?' I replied, staring at my ugly truth.

The round frames made my face look square and in return the square frames made my head appear round. I can't win for losing.

'I see you beginning a new trend – children will arrive to opticians begging for an Oscar special,' pretended the optician.

The mirror was my only sources of honesty and honestly, I'd bully myself. The rims were bigger than the one on a basketball rim. Their temple strap had this unusual quality of changing colour depending on which way the lights struck it.

'I think we have a winner,' said the optician, forcing those horrendous glasses onto my face.

The metal bridge pinched my nasal bone; then its nose pads snapped off, digging into my skin. I can add bifocals to this ever-growing list of enemies.

'A slight adaption is called for; a snout like yours was always gonna be tricky,' dissed the optician, heading into a small workshop.

After twenty minutes of loud drilling, sawing, screwing and gluing he re-emerged. I slipped on the newly modified glasses which fitted all too well. Their lenses were as thick as double glazing.

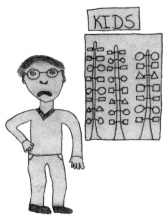

CHAPTER 11

Copy Cat

Yet another week had flown by quite quietly in some degree. I suffered name calling, was pushed down a flight of stairs, chased home by year 11s and now was solely regarded as the haunted one, a picture that since its conception had got positive feedback and been framed and hung above the main hall. Apart from that a pretty average school week.

Our first term swiftly reached its closing stages. Lance and I made a decent pact; find the most obscure areas to hide and, if all else fails, just run. This Friday was known as casual Friday; all children could wear their own clothes. Me, having the world's most glamorous mom, had to be kitted out. She bought new white plimsolls, stonewashed skinny jeans and a turquoise slim fit shirt. I spiked my hair into a sharp quiff feeling fresh, a hint of dad's exclusive cologne, perfection.

'Looking smoking hot, Oscar,' said no one ever. In fact, people couldn't see beyond the glasses. How ironic? People can't look past my eyewear and I can't see through it.

'Four eyes git.'

'Goggle face.'

'Glass head.'

None of these insults were original, only recycled rubbish. I dismissed their remarks; by now they were water off a duck's back.

'Nice threads,' beamed Lance.

'The man makes the clothes, not the other way round,' I responded.

Lance stood in appreciation. 'You're so cool.'

'I work with the many blessings I receive,' I quoted.

'And so wise.'

Little did Lance know all my wise quotations came from a self-help book. You'd be surprised what you find in a charity shop; one man's junk is another man's key to friendship. Lance was solid and dependable, if not an odd character. He wore his socks over his corduroy trousers and owned the longest fringe in history. The fringe was so long he had to part his hair to brush his teeth. But I'm not exactly flushed in the friends department.

We waited besides our first period English.

'Did you complete the essay?' wondered Lance.

'Yes, extra credit too,' I bragged.

'Good, glad I'm not the only one.'

'Why would that be a bad thing?' I asked.

'Learning and doing homework isn't the norm at Winterberry. Teachers set projects just for the sake of the curriculum.'

'Get out of town.'

'No, serious. Look.' Lance opened his backpack showing me his work from Maths, Science and Geography all unmarked.

You could highlight the super cool kids by their timekeeping skills; they'd waltz into lessons all hours of the day. Needless to say, Lance and I were punctual and so far attained 100 per cent school attendances.

The corridor we waited in was long and spacious; it connected all areas of the building. As students and teachers rushed by, they elbowed, kicked and scratched, taking chunks out one another.

'Left hand side, please,' barked the teachers.

Personally, I assume these brainless nitwits couldn't tell left from right. The tiny, weedy and agile year 7s sneaked through gaps between legs, underneath arms and some experimented crowdsurfing.

Crowd surfing phased out as soon as it came in, everyone put this down to the crazy story of Sam Davenport. It's story time folks so gather round. Way back in the year of 1994 a sharp minded Sam Davenport hopped on the shoulders of a year 11, then he laid flat over the blanket of hustling bodies. Excited by riding a wave to class, he relaxed, absolutely ignorant to the pickpockets stealing his wallet, shoes, shirt, coat, trousers, tie and regrettably boxer shorts.

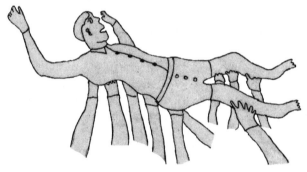

'That'll do me,' he boasted.

Once his bare feet touched ground, he realised what a fatal mistake he made. Kids teased him for days, weeks, months, years and decades. It got to a point where he moved city, but the story of naked Sam stuck like a dodgy tattoo. Take note when riding high; someone's already plotting to knock you off your perch.

'Oh no, the mob, twelve o'clock,' warned Lance.

In every school year there resides a bunch of inbred thugs. Those kids not concerned with education but out for trouble. They hunt in packs. Who do they think they are? Wearing identical football kits, very imaginative, oh oh. My glasses have been located.

'What a spectacular vision I see,' a gang member grinned vengefully.

'Why thank you,' I politely acknowledged.

He ripped the glasses off me, sticking them on. 'How do I look?' He stumbled about acting like a zombie.

'Incredible, can I have my bifocals back?'

'Sharing is caring, selfishness isn't what a friend is.'

'I struggle for sight without them,' I said, trying to gain mercy.

Seeing my anguish incensed his evil traits. He held the glasses in his palm, tempting me.

'Grab it then. You better be quick,' he baited.

I launched my hand forward, too slow. He chucked them to an equally horrible brat. They toyed with me, tossing the specs over my head repeatedly.

'Come on mate, you've had enough fun,' I said, grasping my tightening chest.

These demon children revelled in pleasure. Soon additional kids joined the party. I chased the glasses back and forth as rows of mongrel teenagers flipped, threw and lobbed. I was now out on my feet, breathing shallow, when who should I see marching down the corridor? The figure of Mr Trent surged past. I tugged his arm.

'Sir, Mr Trent,' I shouted.

'Oscar Smart, to what do I owe this displeasure?' he growled.

'They've taken my glasses.'

Mr Trent huffed; my issues weren't on his schedule. However, Headmaster Russell observed from his office. So, he begrudgingly set down his musty-looking caramel briefcase.

'Attention students, this gentleman's glasses seem to have gone walkies,' informed Mr Trent.

'I haven't got them.'

'Me neither, what are glasses?' protested the oh so innocent school kids.

'Look here, I couldn't care less who has them, just that the item returns to its rightful owner.'

The rascal children may not be academically gifted, but they can sense a booby trap. If one kid fessed up, they'd be hit with an automatic suspension.

'Fine, I'm gonna turn away. If Oscar's belongings aren't retrieved every single person will receive a full week's detention.'

As Mr Trent swivelled, the crowd jostled about, disbanding.

'Right, is it back?'

I slipped open my blazer pocket, finding two glass lenses and a crooked frame.

'Crisis over folks. The world is now a safer place,' smiled Mr Trent.

'They destroyed them though, sir,' I argued.

'Nothing is ever acceptable for Oscar Smart. Listen, princess, stop the drama.'

'What drama?'

'He brings trouble to us all sir, nobody bothers him,' blabbed a gang member.

'This is the end of the matter. No more spectacles; we all have glasses to be attending,' shrieked Mr Trent, picking up his briefcase.

'You're hilarious, sir,' praised the gang member.

Am I paranoid? Or is there a total witch hunt going on?

The corridor emptied instantly.

Our English teacher hadn't budged a bit.

'Maybe she's dead," thought Lance.

'Go check,' I instructed.

Lance very slowly poked his head through the door; using my lens as a magnifying glass he stared at her limp body.

'Well, is she, or isn't she?'

Her stomach expanded then deceased in size showing signs of life.

'I think she's catching some zzzz's,' declared Lance.

Our classmates groaned.

'False alarm guys, looks like we do have English,' announced a small girl.

While Winterberry High has its rare blend of bullies and thieves, there has to be one top dog. Mean Dean Jackson fitted the bill. He was brutal and heinous, a child you'd cross the street to avoid. Thankfully, Dean spent the majority of his time with the headmaster, usually for foul-mouthed rants or truancy. When allowed to emerge he ran the year 7 mob like Al Capone. People gravitated to him as flies do to poo. Comparing Dean to poo would be an insult – to poo.

'Deano, good of you to join us,' sweet talked his yes men.

'Yeah, had to come back, was gonna kick me off the school football team otherwise,' he grumbled.

'Liking what you're wearing.'

'Hot stuff,' blushed a couple girls standing in line.

'It's just who I am,' smoothly spoke Dean.

There was a clamouring of students surrounding his space.

'This man's got style and flair,' gloated one of his buddies.

I had to see what the hubbub was about for myself. Dean looked impressive in his white plimsolls, stonewashed skinny jeans and a turquoise slim fit shirt. Oh crap, we're doubles.

'What's this, you copying my swag?' Dean grunted; he went from zero to enraged in a blink.

'Coincidences happen,' I reasoned.

Dean's rugged face frowned, and his red-raw knuckle bones swelled out his fist.

'Knock his block off.'

'Tear him a new one, Dean.'

'Give him a pasting,' encouraged our classmates excluding Lance; come to think of it, Lance hadn't been seen in a while.

'It's only a coincidence, definitely unintentional,' I bartered.

His size 9 plimsolls arrived at my feet. He cracked each knuckle twice. Children formed a barrier around the possible escape points.

'I hate people trying to take the Michael.'

'I thought your name was Dean?' I joked.

He slammed his forearm into my neck, driving me up against a locker with the free hand cocked and loaded. I closed, clenched, crossed and squeezed all my body parts.

'Please! I'm incredibly sorry.'

'Sorry won't cut it. They require blood,' Dean vented.

He launched.

'Wait, Dean, think on it,' said his friend, grabbing Dean's spiteful fist with both hands.

'How else can I settle this?'

The guy took Dean away. They argued and argued.

'You're right, I owe you one for showing me the light,' he apologised.

And there's me implying all Winterberry High attendees are sadistic and depraved people. However, my initial notions were correct. Dean hadn't kicked my head in because one more incident this term would see him expelled. He composed his fury and a bout between us was rearranged for Monday after school. Magnificent, I have a scheduled ass whooping, just a little *something; something* to ponder during our half term break.

CHAPTER 12

Training Days

With a full week's notice ahead of the clash I installed my very own training camp. According to fighters, battles are won and lost in the gym. Proper, preparation, prevents, possible, problems, so I brought Lance to be my chief trainer overseeing strength and conditioning.

I'd travel the short distance to his home, where he'd set up a punch bag and boxing ring made from four broken mop handles and an old washing line. Lance's stern stance had me intimidated. He created a dedicated working attitude and even went to the extremes of producing t-shirts. His pronounced him head trainer, while mine just deemed me the haunted one.

'This is where champions are made,' he motivated.

'Can you teach me how to throw a straight punch?'

Lance blew a whistle assertively. 'Boxing is a sweet science. Footwork, stamina and coordination; we have to master the fundamentals pre-hand.'

'What? Look, I'm in a fight. I want some weapons to keep him off me,' I explained.

He blew the whistle ruthlessly, his cheeks overflowing with air.

'Blow that whistle again and I'll swing for you.'

'Good, grasshopper, anger can aid you,' Lance grabbed a pair of mitts. 'Show me your basic skills.'

I stood square on, slapping his mitt. Shot by shot my confidence grew. I shuffled, bobbed and weaved. Uppercuts, right hooks and jabs all found a home. Then Lance did the most unforeseen action. Boom! He stepped forward, flicking out a faint jab himself. I regressed, using the gloves to cover my head and body.

'Wow, what are you doing?' I asked.

'You think Dean isn't gonna strike back? He'll be all over you like a skin infection.'

Lance didn't pull any punches; he persisted invading my space.

'Stop, I surrender,' I cried.

'Oscar, we must train. Your jab's inaccurate, lacks fizz and pop, Dean'll have you laid out seeing stars.'

Lance knew best; sometimes advice from a friend can put situations in clear view. Since Dean retained massive advantages in power, speed and experience, having Lance as a corner man gave me a puncher's chance.

'All things start from the base up. Are you with me?'

'Yeah, like trees, they always need solid roots,' I said.

'Quick learner. There's hope yet. A sturdy platform is where a majority of force will arrive.'

Lance jerked and twisted my legs, bending them into all types of angles and degrees. Not too narrow, not too far out, not too straight, not too sideways and a slightly raised heel. My golly, sweet science, long ago I came to the conclusion boxers were braindead morons. However, after five minutes of technique drills, I confess there's a certain genius to it all.

'This time turn as you land, bring the punch up through the legs.'

I concentrated diligently, summoning the power from toes to calf up along my thighs. I sent that increasing energy to my stomach then let it blaze a trail down the arm. Pop! The jab snapped. Lance's mitt caved to the pressure applied.

'Easy, champ. Store that aggression, we got a big fight camp organised.'

'Fight camp?'

Lance took off his mitts, opening a journal. 'According to the net, training for a contest can take a minimum of eight weeks. Having this battle on short notice left us pressed time wise.'

'What next?'

'Well champ, discover your new life.'

'I'm dying for a drink, have you got any coke?'

'No fizzy drinks, only water. No sweets, only fruit,' informed Lance.

'That can't work.'

Lance folded his arms. 'Anyone who has ever accomplished greatness had to sacrifice something they love. For your disobedience drop and give me twenty push-ups.'

Although he wanted twenty, six was all my scrawny arms could offer.

'I may still make a man out you yet. Let's go do some roadwork,' inspired Lance.

We hit the streets. I pummelled the pavement with Einstein barking at my heels. Lance rode his bicycle behind, shouting encouragement.

If my fitness levels elevated, who was I to judge? Lance wouldn't accept any lame excuses; after the endurance boosting long runs, he allowed a brief rest period before our afternoon session.

'I can only imagine how Dean's gonna feel being sparked out,' said Lance, setting up a circuit course with cones and a hula hoop.

He invested a lot of effort in my camp. I found it generally petrifying; I'd be duking it out with Dean in under a week. Dean's devious face consumed my thoughts. I saw him in cereal, in lakes, at home and in nightmares.

'I'm a long shot by anybody's estimate.'

'Granted, I wouldn't bet the house on you. But every dog has its day. Now get this down you,' coached Lance, handing me a glass of a gooey yellow substance.

The liquid sloshed up the glass; cracked shells lingered on the surface.

'Four raw eggs. Bottoms up, Oscar,' Lance pinched my nose, tilting the glass.

Gulp! The sloppy, lumpy yolk wobbled past my tongue, sliding towards my throat.

'It's so disgusting,' I heaved.

'Suffer now so the fight will be a cinch.'

'Honestly, in your heart of hearts, reckon I could snatch victory?'

'What does he have that you don't?' asked Lance.

On paper we both had working arms, legs, feet, hands and a head. He was couple months older than me but overall, I matched up favourably.

'Nothing, really,' I replied optimistic.

'Early bird retrieves the worm. Be sharp and precise. Use reflexes and never underestimate shock value.'

'What do you mean by shock value?'

'The element of surprise. Catch your opponent daydreaming and it's Oscar's hand they'll raise,' said Lance, signalling three boys to enter his backyard.

'Who are they?'

'Sparring partners. They're here to mimic Dean's movement and fighting style.'

The lads were giddy in joy. A fight for them was an average daily occurrence.

'Oscar, meet partner one. He'll be super aggressive, in constant attack mode. Don't let up,' advised Lance.

Partner one threw punches in bunches. He didn't target specific places. He fought dirty stamping on my foot.

In seeing his owner being assaulted Einstein barked ferociously. I'd never seen my dog act so violently. However, it was a great sense of comfort knowing someone would stand up for me. To protect my glorified punch bags, I chained Einstein to the fence.

'Stick and move, pick your shots, time it Oscar,' yelled Lance.

I sidestepped his dramatic lunges, landing an effective over-hand right.

'Nice one. Threw it like a lightweight champ,' clapped Lance.

My sparring combatants changed over every three minutes. I welcomed partner two, whose main outline was defence.

'Go on the offence, Oscar. Walk him back, set traps; remember shock value.'

I stalked the second guy, commanding the ring's centre. I pumped a few fake jabs to distract his attention, and then BAM! Straight left closed the case.

'Tremendous! Dean won't know what hit him, ready for round three?'

'No sweat. I'm primed, fast, ruthless, lethal and deadly,' I boasted.

The third partner froze on the ring apron. His timid hands shook the ring post. Old Oscar might've shared unity in this young boy's anxiety. New Oscar two point 0 is a whole different animal.

'Get in here, kiddo. I'll go lightly, gentle taps.'

Training foe three flung his gloves off scared and dashed home.

'Wimp! All right, who's up to challenge the supreme being?'

'I'll skip it for now, thanks,' shied partner two.

Sparring partner one nursed his bruises, quitting the session.

'Is it so hard to get me real rivals? Someone who'll stand toe to toe and bang it out,' I gloated.

'OK, champ, that's enough for one day. Rest up. Take an ice bath,' said Lance, yanking out my gum shield.

'I'm wired. Wish the fight was tonight,' I screamed excitedly.

'Cool it, you're becoming edgy. You've got to control emotions.'

Lance established a solid routine. Monday, Wednesday and Friday included roadwork with sparring. Tuesday and Thursday combined weightlifting and circuit training. I did a record twelve press-ups and sixteen sit-ups. I also cleaned and jerked a fifteen-kilo bag of Basmati rice. By Friday evening I lounged, both physically and mentally spent. On Saturday Lance and I discussed tactics, questioning a variety of scenarios. Sunday totally belonged to public relations. The fight is now less than eighteen hours away.

CHAPTER 13

Social Network

All fights need maximum exposure. In boxing, press conferences are held in lavish hotels. However, a duel between two eleven-year olds probably won't require such recognition, and there's no better place than the internet for free publicity. Tongue Wagger is the only website worthy of holding this important event. Hot topics trending right now are shoes, football and, residing at the top of the tree, Mean Dean Jackson vs. The Haunted One. Speaking to the media for a fighter is as appealing as pulling teeth. You wouldn't see special army commandos chatting to local news broadcasters.

Lance and I sat in his computer room. I don't know how they survive without Wi-Fi. 'Calm, cool, collected. No reason to get hyped,' proposed Lance, switching on his webcam.

The picture was quite grainy; I barely made out their faces. Upon searching the names of people online Dean Jackson didn't appear. Could the bully be running scared?

'Who has got the first question?' I opened up to the committee.

'Dean told me he's gonna break every bone in your body from the neck down. So you'll look like a mummy,' spouted Dean's buddy.

'Listen here dummy, where's your question? Don't you understand how a Q and A works?' I insulted.

'Wow, big mouth. Fine, how do you feel about being beaten to a pulp?'

'Ain't gonna happen. Takes more than one dimwit to take me out.'

'Please, Dean will rip you from pillar to post,' he added.

The in-ring confidence I gained had officially transferred to outright arrogance. I swiftly swallowed another egg elixir.

'Doubtful. In fact, Dean might need to be fitted for crutches, walking stick or better yet a wheelchair.'

'Ease up on giving it the big I am,' panicked Lance.

'Hang back, coach. Let me handle business.'

Lance gawked at the monster he had created.

'Why are you so certain of triumph?' asked a female participant.

I zoomed in the webcam, so my head covered the screen. 'Dean isn't clever enough, nothing between the ears. I'd be surprised if he's got the stones to turn up tomorrow.'

'Stop, man, you'll rile him,' worried Lance.

'And another thing. I'm here doing a public service while he is somewhere eating his snot.'

The thirty- five children logged in consisted of stunned faces. Their jaws hit their keyboards.

'You heard me. Dean is hiding behind his minions, afraid to meet his maker.'

Lance, frustrated and distressed, exited the room.

'Are you on medication, Oscar?' they speculated.

'I take two tablets of faith, one vial of courage, two doses of anger and wash it down with intelligence.'

The people following my conversation online tripled and then tripled a further three times.

'Dean is taller and a more seasoned scrapper; how do intend on combating this?'

'Bigger they are, the harder they fall,' I winked.

'You do fathom you'll be expected to fight for real?'

'Obviously, thicko, I'm entertaining the idea of ending the contest early.'

'Weapons are illegal. At Winterberry High it's mano a mano,' declared the unofficial ref.

'Once my fist graces his skull a single time he'll break down in tears, scrambling away like an infant being left at day-care.'

Our hash tag peaked at six million people globally. The comment board was overloaded with messages like *who is this guy? The boy needs a straitjacket. He must have a death wish. Does he not know Dean is a black belt in karate; kickboxing, Brazilian Jiu jitsu and last week bashed up a fifteen-year-old?* The new information was unsettling. A few rounds in a shabby ring gave me Muhammad Ali's wit and motor mouth, but perhaps not his array of boxing mastery.

'Oscar, I never knew you were a bad boy,' beamed Rachael.

'Lots of sides to Oscar. I'm like a Rubik's cube,' I charmed.

'What, colourful and square?' joked Dean's crew.

'The only colour to be seen will be on Dean when I leave him black and blue.'

Rachael sniggered, 'So daring, my Romeo.'

Did she say Romeo?

'Sort your love affair out later,' yelled the crew.

'Why? Dean's in for it. This was supposedly a convo between two battle-hardened warriors.'

At times the brain loses ownership of your mouth and in these freak situations you may go a tad too far.

'But oh no, Dean is busy breastfeeding or having his mom change his nappy.'

The followers cowered in silence. Lance returned with a pale and bleak exterior; he sagged in his chair.

'You've crossed the line. Made it a family issue,' judged Lance.

'We're fighting regardless.'

'Mothers are forbidden talking points. Grandparents, fathers, sisters, brothers, cousins, aunties and uncles too.'

'I'm not bothered about Dean's loser family.'

'Loser family,' seethed a voice in the background.

'Oh fiddlesticks, zip it Oscar,' fretted Lance.

'I got him shook. Lance, egg me.'

'Don't overdo it.'

'Eggs, man, ASAP. Gotta be in tip-top condition.'

'Your mouth's writing cheques your body's gotta cash,' Dean stormed to the screen; a mammoth vein pulsed in his forehead.

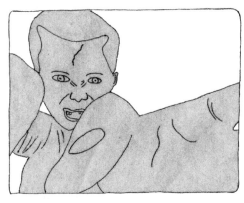

He'd been listening all along. My boasts, brags and cockiness hadn't fallen on deaf ears.

'Well well. Look who decided to show his grotesque face,' I added.

'We don't have to wait for Monday, just give me your location,' blazed Dean.

Lance covered the mic before I could respond. 'Winning the war of words doesn't guarantee similar results in the battle.'

'Nah, I want people to witness the carnage,' I smugly replied.

'Please stop talking, Oscar,' begged Lance.

'I will make mincemeat out of you. Continue yapping and I'll inflict a more vicious beating,' claimed Mean Dean.

'Oh, scary. First I'll slap you silly, then I'll mop the floor with you.'

Dean was at odds. His assurance of a basic beatdown dwindled. He hushed up, glaring into the camera lens.

'What's up, cat got your tongue? Weenie Deanie,' I added.

'Weenie Deanie, classic,' endorsed my growing fanbase.

'Whoever calls me that, I'll bury.'

'Unlikely. You'll be eating through a straw once I pounce.'

'Dean, Oscar is speaking for himself. In no direct way do I condone his behaviour,' explained Lance, distancing himself from my cruel jibes.

'Why are you apologising to this scrubber? If anyone deserves respect, it's me. Dean nicked my image. Deep down I think he idolises me,' I said.

'Got anything to say in response?' asked the enthralled followers.

Dean's status went offline. There's a wise old saying that goes a little something like, if you play with fire, you're gonna get burnt.

'No heart. He's a fraud, a bum, a no good nimrod that'll be dealt with handily. Until tomorrow, fans, goodbye.'

I'd given Dean something to chew on. However, he possessed a spectacular appetite. An appetite for violence, which he would eventually demonstrate.

CHAPTER 14

Mean Dean Jackson Vs. The Haunted One

When fight night arrives, all contenders wrestle with doubt. Training, weight cuts, webcam duty and outlining strategies all for a couple seconds of fisticuffs put me on the verge of meltdown. You realise it's game day and any big proclamations will be displayed as lies, because in competition true winners are declared. The day started as expected; the sun rose, breaking away from the shackling clouds. I ate breakfast and wandered off to school. Now the eggs I digested yesterday caused me short-term memory loss. Did I do a press conference on Tongue Wagger? School kids clocked my arrival. They whooped and hollered; seems Oscar Smart's hot property. Lance would usually wait for me by registration, but today he blitzed me.

'How are you, Lance?'

He walked on, giving me the cold shoulder.

'Yo, Lance.'

'Can't stop,' he mumbled.

I chased him down the corridor. 'Have I done something to offend you?'

Lance pushed me into the boys' toilets so no one would know we were friends. He looked frazzled, checking every cubicle twice over. He then repeatedly pressed the hand dryer while speaking.

'Tell me you're gonna fake an accident, slip on some milk at lunchtime,' whispered Lance.

'Why would I do such a thing?'

'Tongue Wagger! The antics you got up to could see a man killed.'

'A bit of tongue-in-cheek insults, that's how the game is played,' I said.

Lance's dismal gestures affected my optimistic outlook.

'Fill me in; you're probably making a mountain out a molehill.'

'OK. Once the press conference got underway you indulged in saying his father wished he'd been a girl. You carried on posting pictures of a group of kangaroos, stating it was a Jackson family outing. Then went further, explaining why he wasn't allowed to visit his grandparents because one's so ugly it might frighten them to death.'

'I said all that?'

'Wait, there's more. His mother was branded dumb as a door-nail. For an encore you mooned him, telling him to pucker up.'

'You're pulling my leg. I wasn't acting myself. He'll understand, won't he?' I prayed.

'Got pretty heated between the both of you, especially after your picture was reposted a million times.'

'Crikey, what was in those eggs, Lance?'

'Bit of this, bit of that. Soy Sauce and Tabasco.'

'Spices make me hyperactive,' I fussed.

'Mental note taken for the rematch.'

'Should I tell a teacher?'

Lance squeezed my lips together. 'Some things we don't kid about.'

The tough guy figure I posed on screen disintegrated; that's what they call a keyboard warrior. You come across all high and mighty online then get chopped down to size.

'So, how's this milk accident work?'

'You just kept stirring the pot, discussing how the only dentist he saw was on telly,' Lance chuckled.

'Do you see me laughing?'

'I warned, protested and grovelled.'

I flew too close to the sun and paid for it. Lance the head trainer vanished; I needed consoling from a dear friend. 'Pop him with a double jab. I'll see to it that headmaster Russell is notified,' planned Lance.

'What happens if Mr Russell isn't quick? I'll be dead meat.'

Lance's skin tightened as if it was pulled by string, his eyes narrowed brimming with pity. 'Remember head movement, keep the range and no stupid lunges.'

I'm in deep doo-doo; my arms fell limp, joining my legs as faulty body parts.

'Oscar, hold up for twenty seconds. Let me get to class first. We shouldn't associate today,' said Lance, whisking down the hallway.

I went through the day unnoticed, although impending doom circled the atmosphere. Lessons dragged like nobody's business. All I could do was take my licks like a man. Generally, fighters find a way to unwind in a peaceful place to escape the building tension, whether it's walking, talking, singing or listening to calming music. Sadly, Winterberry High didn't suffer fools lightly. Mr Trent's last period Geography got co-main event honours. Other than English Dean and I only shared one subject together, Geography.

Mr Trent read the names off his register.

He reeled off a handful more names, ticking as he progressed. Mr Trent's classroom temperature dropped below freezing, yet the man sweated like a fat man in a sauna. Puddles formed wherever he tottered. His excessive clamminess wasn't the awful factor. At home his wife concocted ghastly sandwiches; sour creams, garlic and spam, on occasions onions, pickles, gherkins and extra strong mature cheddar cheese. Mr Trent's pores acted as vents thrusting his scent around. It lingered in people's clothes for weeks.

'Dean Jackson.'

A sudden flood of boos and jeers accompanied his name.

'Dean Jackson. Dean Jackson?' said Mr Trent peering above his register.

Was he a no-show? Cold feet perhaps. A clash hailed as fight of the millennium could crush a person under the weight of expectation.

'Here, sir,' snarled Dean's hostile voice.

'My man,' smiled Trent.

I spun my head just to gander at the obstacle my opponent posed. Golly. Dean zoned out the class; he channelled all his fierce energy towards me. Dean had added size to his frame, filling out across the shoulders, arms and chest. Now bulking up meant he'd utilize power for maximum damage from minimal shots. Dean's wicked eyes followed me; they were haunting. I switched seats a dozen times, but he remained vigilant.

'Hellfire, I'm a goner Lance,' I cried.

'Oscar Smart.'

My name was greeted with a chorus of hearty cheers. I'd earned a cult following, little old me the fans favourite.

'Here, sir,' I replied.

'Mr Popularity, aren't we?' said Mr Trent.

'Mind over matter, yeah? He presents a ruthless, hateful and uncompromising character.'

'Where's the but? Tell me there's something to hang my hat on.'

Lance mulled a positive aftermath. 'Wounds heal and broken bones can be mended.'

'Good, I've got rehabilitation in the works.'

'All those days at home with your feet up? Oscar, you've got it made.'

Lance forgot the fact my house is associated with terms like crumbling, caving, abysmal and disastrous wreck.

Minutes ticked loudly; the seconds taunted me by drifting away rapidly.

Hoopla ignited as my classmates debated how the grudge bout would unfold.

Mr Trent normally stayed behind his desk engaged in playing solitaire on the computer. Chattering about Dean and Oscar's fight repeatedly perked his attention. Curious, Mr Trent shut his laptop, seeing Dean still firmly locked on me, the unfancied rival.

He roamed around the room, sloshing as sweat clogged up his shoes. Kids dealt with Mr Trent's stench in many ways, covering their noses, spraying deodorant and dropping pot pourri into his coat pockets. Day by day he'd dig out jasmine, rosemary and lavender leaves. 'Where are all these smelly plants coming from?' he whined.

Mr Trent sat in the vacant chair next to Dean; they communicated subtly, shielding their mouths. Out of everyone I knew at Winterberry Mr Trent would've have been the last person I expect to play peacemaker. Both guys shook hands, reducing my anxiety.

'Oscar, Stinky Trenty has saved the day,' grinned Lance.

'Thankfully! I was crapping myself,' I said.

'Think I'm more relieved than you are.'

'Why? I was doing the jousting.'

'I want to clear my conscience,' Lance said timidly.

'Lay it on me.'

'Those sparring partners you manhandled are what the boxing profession call dummy men.'

'Dummy men?' I said.

'Boxing coaches bring in bums and novices to aid a fighter's belief. No hard feelings.'

'How could I be mad at you, mate?'

Lance did what he thought was best and thanks to Mr Trent's good nature the fight of the millennium IS CANCELLED! Sorry for any inconvenience.

And so, the day fizzled out; the bell alerted us of home time and children left in an orderly fashion. Of course they did – this is Winterberry High we're talking about, not some upper class prep school.

Dean had me secured in his crosshairs; he thrashed past my table. 'Time to face the music,' he declared.

My knobbly knees jangled in despair. I speculated on the conversation he had with Mr Trent.

'Chin up, Oscar,' chortled Mr Trent.

'What, sir? I want you to go out there and break a leg.' He launched me out of his classroom.

'Shucks! Sugar plums!' I crumbled.

'Jab, jab and grab! I'll squeal like a little piggy to Mr Russell,' said Lance, dashing away.

Due to the superfight's popular demand, it was relocated from the regular spot of behind the bike sheds to the teacher's car park. You might be assuming a school car park, surely it's gonna be crammed, but teachers evacuated Winterberry High as if it were a fire drill.

I strolled down the corridor, dragging my feet. Pure silence escorted me to the bout. There are umpteen examples of tiny unknown prospects going on to shock the world. Rocky v Apollo Creed. In the bible David takes down the fearsome Goliath. Maybe it's time for Oscar Smart to write his name in the history books.

Roughly three thousand kids log-jammed the car park. Children owning different uniforms made the trip down. I heard Scottish, Irish and Welsh accents being spoken. The intoxicated fans created a circular ring. Dean cold-heartedly stood dead centre. I gradually entered the hotbed environment. The crowd erupted baby footstep by baby footstep.

'How the rich have fallen, Oscar boy,' shouted a delighted fan near the front row.

I turned to see who yelled the abuse, Timothy, my once bestie, now another bystander here to observe the destruction.

I headed straight towards Dean. No point in sitting on the back foot; people remember aggression. Lance better be in position.

The Haunted One v Mean Dean Jackson is now upon us. For those of you unfortunate enough to not have a ringside seat the megafight will also be streamed online at www.thehauntedonevme-andean.com and Tongue Wagger have a video feed too.

Dean and I connected eye to eye; a classic staredown ensued. Peering into his face I sensed the agitated state he lived in; his face twitched. The magnitude dawned on him.

'Don't blow it, Deano.'

'A loss like this would be an outrage, unforgiveable,' judged his beastly crew.

We backed up a couple paces. I bounced on the balls of my feet. Dean loosened up, jigging about on the spot.

'Let's have it then,' barked Timothy.

The crowd immersed us in excited screams. I fought out of a southpaw stance, being left-handed. For future reference approximately ten per cent of the world are lefties. Dean was cagey, keeping a high guard. I rotated clockwise then anticlockwise. Lively, Lance, he's not gonna wait all day.

'Fight! Fight! Fight!' ranted the crowd.

Dean stuck his chin out; that's when something triggered in my mind. Element of surprise. I never accepted his invitation. Instead I gave him a swift dig in the stomach. He stumbled back astonished, if not actually hurt.

'Go on lad,' they projected.

I flashed out a double jab, planting one on above his eyebrow. Kids looked bewildered. Dean still didn't unleash his offence. Pop! Pop! I faked a headshot, landing one in his sternum. I dominated every aspect of the one-sided affair. I won the jab exchange, took centre of the ring and he ate my jab like cheese on toast.

'It's a fix, someone's paid him to take a dive,' fumed the crowd.

Dean had a suspicious glance towards Mr Trent's window. I activated another piston right hand, which he excellently slipped. My upper cut missed by acres. He ducked, dodged and shoulder rolled my relentless assault. Beating up thin air wasn't in my fight plan.

'Great defensive adjustment,' cheered Dean's buddy.

Say the fight ended now I'd have a won on points. But Dean sent a whopping right hook with pinpoint accuracy. Bang! It rocketed off my nose. Dizzy, dazed and dumbstruck I staggered. My legs resembled jelly. He then returned my body blow with interest. Wallop! He wore my stomach as a glove for a couple seconds.

Just fight back, Oscar. I swung for the fences, throwing seven punches; six went astray and I landed one thunderous hit on my own eye.

'Idiot, he's trying to knock himself out,' laughed Timothy.

Dean threw a nasty leg kick, sweeping me into the air. He closed proceedings winding up for the legendary booming windmill, which he had demolished many opponents with. His missile fist gathered momentum as I attempted to avoid it.

'Skedaddle! Mr Russell,' yelled the lookout.

Three thousand kids shimmied up trees, dove through bushes and hopped gates to evade being linked to the bout.

Lance came in the nick of time.

'Dean, get in my office immediately!' demand Mr Russell.

Dean's missile deactivated, arriving back to its home base.

Out of nowhere Mr Trent cropped up.

'Beat me to the punch, Mr Russell. I saw this ruckus begin and promptly came to investigate,' Mr Trent lied.

'Very well, I can take over from here,' said Mr Russell, grabbing Dean. 'Think it's best you look for a new school. You may be a fabulous football player, but violence, Mr Jackson, can't be glossed over.'

'I insist, headmaster, there are three sides to every story. Yours, theirs and the truth,' smiled Mr Trent.

I took my cuts and bruises to the principal's headquarters. He interviewed us one by one. I explained the whole kit and caboodle, everything from identical clothing to the contest itself. I slightly adapted my choice words on Tongue Wagger.

Dean entered second. I spied, peeking through a crack in the door.

Ringside judges all gave Dean the verdict. On balance boxing is a hit and don't get hit sport. My numbers read twenty-two punches thrown and a lousy four connected, while Dean landed an impressive six for six. However, I'd like to think I did myself proud.

Lastly Mr Trent told his version of events. Just before he walked into Mr Russell's room, he and Dean shared a passing glance.

'Pieces are in place,' Dean suggested.

'Time to bring it home,' stated Mr Trent, leaving the door wide open.

'It erupted into chaos! Mr Smart lashed out, a whipping jab combination rocking Dean to his very being. Oscar was an animal, sitting down on his punches, sending spiteful blasts to the midriff.

Dean howled in pain, blocking a shot. The Haunted One, as he is named because of his obsession with the devil, wouldn't be denied. He beat Dean like a mallet tenderizes steak. Pow! Boom! Bam! Punishing attack after attack. Oscar's sick.'

What a load of hogwash!

'Always good to have the law on your side,' Dean smirked ear to ear.

'When I reached the car park Dean had Oscar on his knees. Explain,' said Mr Russell, not completely sold on Mr Trent's story.

'Lucky punch. Oscar bombarded him, totally self-defence,' he implied.

Mr Russell summoned all three of us into his office.

'Is this true, Oscar? Did you throw the first shot?'

'Yes, but only due to the fact . . . '

Mr Russell looked disappointed. Dean had an impenetrable case. I was considered the sadistic criminal.

'You seemed a good egg. A real student who took pride in learning. Now to know you're a savage brute leaves me baffled.'

'Sir, I'm terribly sorry.'

'Legally I've got to suspend you indefinitely until a full-blown report is completed.'

'Quite harsh, headmaster. It's his first significant incident. And I'll testify Oscar's work is exemplary, he's an A grade pupil,' said Mr Trent.

'How would you discipline him in a fair manner?'

'One hundred hours of detention.'

Dean beat me to the bone and Mr Trent picked at them.

'Reasonable enough. Will you see to it he meets his obligation?' agreed Mr Russell.

'If it's the last thing I do,' confirmed Mr Trent.

CHAPTER 15

Einstein

Life had become a humbling experience – outfoxed by the school bully, who's in cahoots with a dictator of a teacher. I dreaded going back Tuesday, Wednesday, Thursday and Friday. The internet was rife with remarks and photos of Dean peppering me. I had almost reached the end of my tether with Winterberry's antics. The sorry excuse for an education, next door neighbours playing heavy metal disrupting my sleep, a bedroom so small you had to change clothes on the landing and waking up to shower in super cold water crowned this hellhole.

There were only a few activities that brought me joy, one of which was Einstein. Dogs are supposed to be man's best friend. Einstein became my only mainstay comrade. He was a Beagle breed cloaked in wonderful golden fur on his face and back with a white underbelly. We rescued him from a pound several years ago. One glance into those marvellous brown eyes that yearned for love entranced us. Pets are more than just animals; they're there through the torrid times, ready to play and uplift spirits. Einstein doesn't understand my pain – walkies, treats and tennis balls are his sole aim. He rushed into the kitchen, yanking his lead down, barking in an enthusiastic way. 'Patience, boy,' I spoke firmly.

Einstein crouched at my feet, obeying his master. I gave him a biscuit for his loyalty.

'Good boy. Now stay.'

I used a frozen pack of peas to compress my reddening eye. On a high note I have pillows for fists, so a black eye was unlikely and the rest of my scars were covered by clothes.

With damage control addressed I collared Einstein, attaching his lead and leaving for the local fields.

Moments of harmony whilst watching my dog chase the tennis ball. His incredible energy kept my glimmer of happiness alive.

'Go fetch, Einnie.'

His tail wobbled excitedly as he raced along the grass, snatching the bouncing ball. An hour or so would pass briskly; I longed for these light-hearted times to last. But Winterberry comes with its pack of cast and characters already included. The local field is where the who's who of dog owners came to walk their protectors. Animals built and bred for annihilation: diabolical illegal Pitbull terriers, American Bulldogs and giant Mastiffs used this field as their personal toilet. Pooper scoopers and doggie bags weren't the done thing, so sidestepping the cluttered dog faeces took guile.

Einstein roamed free and unrestrained. That couldn't be said for the other monsters; they were detained by chains, ropes and steel bars held together with screws and bolts. Owners proudly stood in fondness of their hulking creatures. Some fools once made a ridiculous decision like unclipping the muzzle of a resident bad boy Pitbull named Terror. He eagerly detected freedom, a gust of natural air grazing his glistening teeth. Terror's boss presented himself as commander. However, if you train a killer you receive a killer. iron chain loops strained as Terror applied enormous force and the weakest link broke the chain. What unravelled over a minute involved seven cop cars, four helicopters, two paramedics and several hundred stitches to resolve the hectic consequences. As of now drama was at a minimum, the leashed devil dogs walked unassumingly.

Today Dean and his Dean team made a special impromptu appearance. He had come to gloat. Rachael and Phoebe mingled with the triumphant group. Einstein was a people dog; he adored affection.

'That's a lovely shiner.'

'You were in sparkling form,' praised Phoebe.

Dean held Phoebe's hand. Oh well, I won't lose any sleep over it.

'We have no issues here,' I said, extremely annoyed.

'You're not requiring a rematch, Oscar?' Dean sniggered.

His entourage took the cue to laugh too.

'I'm just walking my dog.'

'As you were, mate.'

'Einstein, get here, boy.'

The group looked at each other strangely, as if someone had just farted in their presence.

'Einstein? Who calls a dog Einstein?' asked Dean.

'Named after Albert,' I clarified.

They all simultaneously shrugged.

'So, he is called Albert?' guessed Dean.

'I see it. It's like when you call William Billy instead or Bob for Robert,' wrongly explained his friend.

'No, Albert Einstein, the German born physicist,' I replied.

'Who?' his friend wondered.

Usually I'd go into an in-depth account of why Albert is one of the greatest minds ever, though the rigmarole of dumbing down quantum mechanics, atoms and subatomic particles wouldn't have helped.

'He was a genius.'

'Who was a genius?' said adrift Rachael, staring deeply into her handheld mirror.

These thickos were giving me a migraine.

'Einstein, now,' I instructed.

The Beagle hurried towards us, tennis ball wedged in his gob.

'Release.'

Einnie dropped the ball straight away.

'One devoted dog you got yourself,' admired Dean.

'He's well trained, aren't you, boy? Yes you are,' I said, stroking his face.

'Get a room,' replied Rachael.

Dean saw the way Einstein respected, loved and worshipped me. He grinned. I gathered our relationship reminded him of his ghastly crew of bootlickers.

Specks of rain began to hit the floor; various black clouds crept over the horizon, hunting down the sun.

'Let's get you home.'

As I went to hook Einstein's lead, Dean picked up the bright yellow tennis ball. He waved it about, exciting the dog. Einstein wiggled out of my grasp, intrigued by his toy.

'Want me to throw it doggie?'

'Dean, I gotta take him inside before it buckets down. Once his coat gets damp he's a nightmare to dry.'

Einstein yelped, thrilled.

'Okay boy,' Dean wiped his massive hands dry then gripped the ball intently. He had that venomous twinkle in his eyes.

Einstein yapped, yelled and howled.

'Hurl it man, see how far you can throw it,' commanded Phoebe.

Guys will do almost anything and everything to impress their sweetheart. Dean clinched the ball thrusting it across the greying sky.

'Watch him work.'

Einstein leaped giddily, fixated on the round object he treasured.

'He's a determined fella,' said Dean.

'Einstein, no, bad dog!' I yelled with an owner's displeasure.

The dog kept plugging away; my desperate cries were thoroughly ignored. The ball touched down on the tarmac path spanning the entire park. Einstein's paws rattled against the surface. His desire for the toy was unwavering. I viewed cautiously as the dreary clouds dispensed its supply of rain.

'Careful, boy! Careful,' I screeched, following my canine companion.

The ball collected water, becoming big, fuzzy and heavy. It slowed down in phases. Einstein reduced his speed too. Then, suddenly, the tennis ball kicked up out of a ditch, planting itself dangerously on the white central markings in the road.

'Einstein, don't. I'll get it.'

I was about twenty feet away from the road. Einstein wagged impatiently; he glared at the ball, then me and then the ball once more. Finally, he barked a mellow bark as if he was apologising for his defiance. By this time local nuisance Mr Lang zipped down the street on his quad bike. Einstein strayed off the pavement. Mr Lang's quad bike engine reverberated, giving off the illusion it was further away. I came to a crestfallen standstill. Einstein froze, seeing his destiny in Mr Lang's bike. Fortunately, Mr Lang used his machine's amazing agility, cocking the bike sideways onto its two wheels skimming Einnie's grateful face.

'Want to get him on a leash, kid,' wrangled Mr Lang, hitting the revs.

Cats are said to have nine lives. So, how many do dogs get? Einstein clutched his ball.

'Lucky escape there, Oscar,' said Dean.

Dean and his servants sauntered back to whatever hole they crawled out of. As Einstein made his way back, the same quad bike returned doing the rounds.

This time the rider wasn't so nimble; he used his obese tummy to steer while wolfing down a sausage roll. Wham! Einstein catapulted, reaching lofty heights. His body bashed the tarmac. The fat blimp didn't stop either, he just flicked up his hoodie and hightailed away.

'That ended a bit ruff,' expressed Dean, displaying no sensitivity.

'You're a funny man, hilarious,' glorified his gang.

I gently stroked Einstein. His tail no longer shimmered; his body lay cold in the rainstorm. November 1st marked the day I officially lost my faint ambition of a resolution. My gut wrenched in agony. Take the poison of chomping down a handful of Cubes, multiply it by a factor of a thousand and you're getting there. Mom and dad comforted me. Einstein, may you be safe in doggie heaven.

'You can have any pet you wish. Be exotic and adventurous as possible,' said dad.

'It's OK. I'm fine. Everybody dies,' I replied, slouching upstairs.

'Give him time to adjust,' requested mom, keeping father from pursuing me.

Losing my lovely Beagle dog was the final straw. In Winterberry, crying is frowned upon. However, throughout the night I depleted and drained my tear ducts, shedding every last drop of fluid. I near enough cried my eyes dry, to where blinking became a monumental task. I will not tolerate this anymore. So I made a very rash but unforgettable decision.

CHAPTER 16

Wagging It

I'd gotten more than I bargained for, stripped of my wealth, dignity, any shred of pleasure and the beloved pet whose name shall not be spoken. I simply didn't have the mettle to hack another day of misery. I evaluated a few available actions to see which suited me best. I decided to skip the whole learning process to take up truanting.

Who needs school anyway? OK, my studies will suffer. I won't go to University. The job prospects dwindle and I'll never run my own sweet company and wipe Mr Sugar off the face of the earth for what he did to my family. In the long run wagging, it wasn't a concrete solution. If every time I have a dilemma I bolt, what does that say about Oscar Smart? Coward, quitter, sensitive, but Winterberry terrified me. No real friends apart from Lance, teachers and students conniving sinister plots to demolish my spirits. The bad outweighed the good. I'm sticking to my guns and wagging it.

There are many classic ways to play truant. The home grown, which consists of using a hot water bottle to heat up your forehead, and swallow chilli powder; so, when a thermometer is placed in your mouth it spikes to boiling point. The drawback to this method is pretending to be ill limits your options to staying in bed sipping soup.

The fool at school is an instant favourite. You pack a change of clothes in your bag, wake up normal time, eat breakfast and leave home as usually. However, once out the door you switch from uniform to casual wear and the day is yours. Fool at school, it's the only way.

'Have a fantastic day at school, Oscar. Learning is vital,' waved mom.

'Righty ho,' I said dishonestly.

From 9am till 3.30pm I could do as I pleased with no one to boss me about. Six and a half hours of bliss. What should I do first? With my free travel pass I rolled into the city centre. I dissected my day up into three structures; the initial couple of hours to be wasted in the shopping centre, part two I'd stroll down my old neighbourhood, then lastly, I'll wander along the canal, taking the longest route home.

Winterberry shopping centre was a drama-filled zone. The building complex harboured discount stores opposite discount stores. "Cheap as Chips", "Best Bargains'" and "Plenty for Pennies" were all businesses plying a massive trade. Adults developed childlike attitudes, fighting and biting over knockdown oven chips and blackcurrant squash.

'I saw it first.'

'Let go or I'll break it off.'

Rampant shoplifting meant metal detectors and security was beefed up. Thieves on countless occasions fled for exits; guards wrestled them with chokeholds or leglocks. The cat and mouse game between villain and law enforcement is an endless war. Women brought buggies without babies to cram in goods. Men made fake stomachs out of papier mache, slipping garments in the hollow space inside.

I swapped out my ugly uniform and melted into the mass of civilians. Poor tribes have a name for it – window shopping, where a person unable to afford expensive items looks and admires without purchasing. I tried on some designer combinations. A woman sat on a rectangular couch waiting for a cousin with a dozen bags. I experienced a knee-jerk reaction.

'Mom, can I have this one?' I asked the unsuspecting lady.

'Excuse me?' she said.

Embarrassed, I swiftly departed the store.

The shopping complex began to liven up and customers flooded the main area. To my surprise and dismay twenty to thirty children entered the centre. I glanced at them from afar, spotting Lance among the grubby brown Winterberry High uniforms. Mr Trent set his class on a data collecting project doing a survey on who shops where and who buys what.

'Right brats, you have approximately two hours to gather information to fill your sheet. Reconvene here at half past eleven. If you need me, I'll be at the all you can eat breakfast bar,' instructed Mr Trent.

The kids split hastily. They found the nearest bin, dumped their sheets and went about their business.

Being caught wagging it by Mr Trent would be unbearable. I bypassed my classmates in the game shop and those rare geeks in the gadget store. Dean and his groupies were checking out new football boots. I blew by female students dossing in the clothing department too. What was I worried about? Most Winterberry pupils didn't know who I was. Mr Trent had been wrangling with workers in the breakfast bar about how many free refills he'd taken.

'That's absolute slander, I'm well within my rights to a refill,' shouted Mr Trent.

I sneaked a peak from behind a perfume stall.

'Pardon? I don't like what you're inferring,' said an irate Mr Trent.

I continued to observe his theatrics then a hand graced my shoulder.

'Oscar Smart?' questioned the voice.

I hesitantly turned around.

'Lance, you had me squirming,' I fretted.

'What are you thinking? Why weren't you at school?'

'I'm ditching. Taking my life back. I ain't coming back either.'

'You're being stupid, what you gonna do for the next five years? Once the truancy police get in contact with your parents they'll be prosecuted,' said Lance.

'There's no such thing.'

Lance pulled me out of the view of Mr Trent, who persisted to argue.

'Trust me, Oscar, they'll be taken to court and could even face jail time.'

'I detest Winterberry High. I'll wag it until I come up with an idea.'

'Tell your parents. Explain what's happening.'

'Who am I, some baby blabbing to mommy and daddy?' I replied.

Lance shrugged. He knew I was heading down a dark road; nonetheless he distracted Mr Trent long enough for me to make my getaway.

I left the centre earlier than expected. Five hours still remained. With Lance's statement ringing fresh in my ears, I needed to clear my head. I skipped returning to my old stomping ground; holding on to the past wouldn't solve my present or future. Bunking off school seems exciting and daring at first, but after a while you realise there's not much to do.

I slowly ambled my way to the canal, dipped under the bridge and chilled on the pathway. The canal air felt cleaner and natural, unpolluted by urban factories producing sickening gases. A stream of positivity dominated my body. The pure oxygen reached deep inside, enlightening me. Tonight I'll plead for a transfer to a different school. My predicament now ironed out, I rounded off my day playing a game of skimming. I clipped pebbles off the canal water; the ripples got larger as I got the hang of things. The motion of pebbles skidding across the surface annoyed the quacking ducks.

'Quack! Quack!'

It amused me, adding a little humour to otherwise another dour day. I flipped a rock, creating a gigantic splashing.

'Oi! Cut your clowning out,' screamed a grainy voice from inside a bush.

The shock of having company perplexed me. A hand bedecked in boils and blisters launched out of a cluster of nettles and attempted to abduct me. I teetered back; my heel tipped, shifting my momentum. Whirling and swirling went the arms, achieving no sense of balance.

Swash! Dunk!

The dank, greasy water swamped me. That wasn't all; a brace of miffed ducks progressed, quacking at the ready. Beaks were displayed, sharp and malicious. I'd get a first-hand glimpse of what the ugly duckling treatment was. They swam; I thrashed against the water, kicking up litres of liquid.

'Quack! Quack!'

I lunged for some weeds to pry myself out but they came apart in my hand. Then straight from the nettles came out a scruffy, unwashed and murky man; he latched onto my arm, tugging me to safety.

'Thank you, kind sir,' I blessed.

'You'll know better than to disturb a man when he's taking a nap,' squeaked the dusty-looking man.

'I didn't mean to disturb you. I'm just trying to kill time.'

The hobo stood glaring at my soaked garments. 'You're a wee nipper. Why aren't you at school, sonny Jim?'

Sometimes it's easier talking to a complete stranger about your complicated story than a loved one.

'I'm done with school for the time being,' I explained.

'Never a wise concept, leaving education early. You wouldn't take a pie out the microwave half cooked, would you?'

He parted a batch of tall nettles that not only were stinging plants, but also acted as his front door.

'Are you homeless?' I asked.

'Depends on which way look at it. The world is my home. I go where I want, when I want. I've been nesting here the past year. Now wipe your feet.'

There were hundreds of strong branches erected into a triangle, perfectly constructed, to protect him from outside predators. The scrubber unzipped his tent. His gaff was immaculate and larger than originally thought.

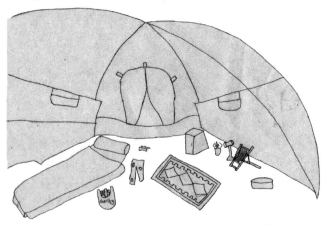

He owned a portable gas cooker and a cooler full of food. We huddled up in his living room. He switched on a lamp, brightening the place up a bit.

'Why do you have the hump?' he wondered.

'It's Winterberry High. They've reduced me to a sad case.'

'Oh, Winterberry. That makes a world of sense,' he shook his head, conceding. 'Takes me back to my younger days in which I made one dumb choice.'

'You went to Winterberry High too?'

'For about six months. I wasn't a heavy hitter, just a regular Joe, Billy no mates. Did my work and avoided problems.'

'So, what happened to you?'

His silence engaged me. I became eager to hear his biography. His filthy lips trembled and rusty crumbs dropped out his patchy beard. However, all those disgusting features paled in comparison to the main story.

'I attempted to crowdsurf back in 1994,' he wailed; tears spilled out of his face. They turned black and brown, merging with his skin.

'Are you Sam?'

'They still retell my horrid tale. Two decades have whistled by. Can't I catch a break?' he crumbled.

'Everyone said you left the city.'

'I bounced from school to school, but little Sammie trailed me like a ghostly shadow. At sixteen I ran away from home, living off nature.'

Was I staring into my mirror image? Bullying is a brutal biz; it shattered my heart to witness this grown man weeping over a childhood memory.

'How do I beat them? Ignoring them isn't the answer.'

The tramp wiped his drenched face on a blanket.

'The best revenge is epic success. Display confidence; rise above their childish pranks. Graduate top of the class, then go on to be wealthy and healthy.'

'I need a quicker justice. I want them to feel anguish, head-aches, diarrhoea and vomiting. Vengeance for Einstein,' I seethed.

'Wow. Who this Einstein fella?'

'My former pet.' I quivered on speaking his name.

'There might be one woman who can give you vindication.'

'Let's head out. Where is she? These imbeciles will rue the day they met Oscar Smart,' I cackled an evil cackle; it felt rude not to.

The homeless man whispered. 'Midnight tonight. Bring me a packet of tobacco, one gallon of diesel and a bottle of single malt for me. Mrs Doovoo only does favours for presents.'

'But I'm eleven! To buy cigarettes and booze you have to be eighteen.'

'Where there's will there's a way.'

Tonight's the night Dean, Phoebe, Rachael and Mr Trent will realise for every action there's a reaction.

CHAPTER 17

The Freaks Come out at Night

I abandoned plans to surrender and opt out of Winterberry. Instead I selected the low road which included retribution. That evening I bunged my soggy clothes in the tumble dryer. Then after eating dinner I contemplated ways of getting the items Mrs Doovoo required. I had sufficient funds, but my baby face highlighted how youthful I was.

Anyone got any ideas? I'm dumbfounded unless I age seven years in the next three hours. This called for some invention. A tiny hurdle like being legally underage to purchase alcohol disrupted my lust for payback. Whichever shop I entered it's probable they'd ask for I.D. At eight o'clock father took a shower before work; he'd leave his wallet and phone on the dresser draw. Mom resided in the lounge watching her favourite romcom for the billionth time.

OK, let's run through the basic facts. Mom's film lasted a mind numbing two hours ten. Dad's personal grooming session is the stuff of legend – I'll be generous and say he'll take a snappy half an hour. I excused myself from the lounge.

'You're gonna miss the best part,' stated mom.

'I'll live,' I said.

I slinked upstairs, very wary of each creaking step. Because of our dodgy plumbing system water sprinkled and spouted in miniscule volume. In saying that, father always spoke about water bills remaining sky-high. Anyway, I slipped open the door to the master bedroom. Father sang off-key as his shower flipped from roasting hot to freezing temperatures. I got one shot at it. Filtering through father's wallet I looked for something that remotely resembled me. Credit, debit and membership cards didn't state a date of birth. I searched every compartment, then a flash of pink dazzled me. I pulled out his plastic driving license and, since father passed his test at seventeen, the similarities were startling.

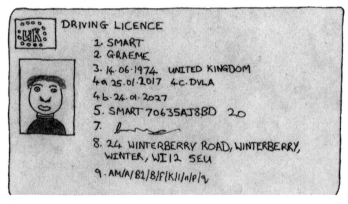

The fleeting shower totally shut down.

'I despise this whole forsaken house,' moaned dad.

I replaced his wallet in exactly the same position.

Once the robbery had been fulfilled, I finished watching the movie with mom. No matter how many times mom views this chick flick she can't refrain from weeping.

'Never gets old. They don't make them like they used to,' she blubbered.

As the end credits rolled dad shuffled off to work.

'Later, Daddio,' I smiled.

His orange car clunked, trundling over our busted-up driveway.

Mother switched her attention to me. 'Think we need to have a heart to heart.'

Recently without the ability to buy beautiful gifts galore, she changed her entire parenting approach.

'So, what's going on in Oscar's world?'

'Making the best of a bad situation, like dad said, school work,' I replied.

'You know you can talk about absolutely anything, even Einstein, love,' mom spoke tenderly.

'He was a glorious dog,' I fended off dwelling on him.

'You were glued at the hip,' pressed mom.

My emotions bubbled inside; his sweet yelping bark, the flapping of his tail and magnificently shining brown eyes. 'Losing a pet is part of the maturing experience.'

'You are taking it far better than I did. When my parrot Bernard croaked, I grieved his passing for eternity.'

We were connecting on a more spiritual base. But revenge is a dish best served cold. Stay the course, Oscar: heartless, callous and uncompromising.

'What doesn't kill you makes you stronger,' I quoted.

I left mom with her bewildered expression.

***

By eleven o'clock mother retired to her sleeping quarters and dad's graveyard shift was well underway. It's time for me to take matters into my own hands. Then I can officially even the score with Winterberry High's gruesome foursome. Donning a shirt and tie I strode to the local petrol station. During the night, the city comes alive; freaks and creeps roam the streets. Women drunk as a skunk stagger, walking wonkily into glass doors, unbeknownst to them. The comical part was females start out flawlessly prancing from nightclub to wine bars in strapping six-inch heels. Then by the night's end they wander about barefoot, unable to walk or talk properly. Men were by no means model citizens. Males resorted to childish gags, tying a naked friend to a lamp post. As for the rest, they were either holding the hair of a girlfriend puking into a dumpster or spilling kebabs along the pavement. For the entire bizarreness going on people found me the peculiar one, clutching my jerry can.

'Aren't you getting smashed, mate?' said a man reeking of alcohol.

I sensed he thought I was his buddy from way back when. He'd repeated the statement Liverpool, like I'd know what he means.

'Exceptional night, unbelievable so it was,' he proclaimed before necking another beer.

'Yeah, no doubt,' I replied, backtracking.

I marched on past the disturbing adults. A lot of street activity happened; my head was on a constant swivel. Grumpy taxi drivers dealt with annoying clubbers who opted not to pay. Yelling and foul language turned the air blue while the stars hid behind the oval moon as if displeased. I hurried. The petrol station was set to close for 11.30pm. I increased my speed with the jerry can tucked under my arm.

'Oi, sunny boy, there you are,' said a spooky voice emerging from a van.

'Are you talking to me?' I said loudly, catching the eye of a bouncer.

'Of course. Your father's tearing his hair out,' the man slowed his van to where it just rolled along at my pace.

'He knows I'm missing?'

'Definitely, he sent me to bring you home lad. So hop in,' the man requested, opening his passenger side door.

A strange man in the dead of night offers you a lift, weird right? Here's how you should handle it. Automatically decline respectfully. Memorise vehicle make, model, number plate and any special features the driver may have. Find a well-lit public area full of pedestrians and call the police.

'You said my dad sent you, what's his name?'

The man flicked his cigarette butt. 'Dad to you. Look, it is all hush-hush in my line of work. Names aren't a priority,' he answered.

'How about my name, they'd at least tell you that?'

He wound down the window completely and stretched his torso out. He wore this curly blonde wig and sunglasses at the tip of his nose which covered his entire face.

'Look, I got popping candy, chocolate bars, crisps and pop,' he said, attempting to boost his chances.

The van had been adapted; there wasn't a handle on the passengers' side and the license plates were removed also. He glanced in his side mirror.

'Mate, you won't get into trouble. Now move it, pronto,' flecks of urgency consumed his tone.

The scenario shook me deep. He became anxious and threatening. I heard a siren piercing the airwaves, and so did he. It subdued him slightly.

'For the last time, jump in. I can't possibly eat all these delicious sweets,' he dangled the confectionery frantically.

Two officers on the prowl stood near the street corner.

'Officer!' I whistled.

'Have it your way, kid,' grumbled the man.

The white van brimmed up a cloud of dust and scarpered away. Abduction skilfully avoided, I scurried to the first available pump. Sam said I needed one gallon of diesel. I squeezed four and a half litres of the flowing liquid, costing me five pound eighty. The sleepy woman behind counter fought her eyelids. She rocked forward, banging her head against the counter.

'Pump number six, please,' I said confidently.

She rang me up on the register with her eyelids almost shut. 'Do you need any other services?'

'Sure, a bottle of single malt and some bacca.' Bacca? Loads of Winterberry alum commonly referred to tobacco as bacca.

She floundered off her stool, picking up the two items. Nervous droplets of sweat ran down my spine.

'Got some identification?'

'One moment please,' I said politely.

'All sorts try it on. Sunday I had a seven year old hit me up for lighter fluid and a lads' mag.'

'The way of the world, kids aren't like us older generation.' I slid the driving license under the metal tray.

Sounding old and wise brought her on song. She squinted at my photo. I smirked.

'Let me get you a bag,' she said.

'That'll be grand.'

Jerry can in my left hand, green plastic bag containing one fine single malt and twenty-five-gram packet of tobacco in the right, I trekked through a field leading to the canal. Unleaded fuel sloshed about in the jerry can; it was so awkward to carry and kept whacking me in the leg. I developed a sharp pulsating pain in my shoulder. I switched hands to lessen the burden. I endured it for as long as possible. Once I no longer had the strength to hold it, I decided to pop the can down for a quick rest bite.

Maybe a swig of single malt to restart my powerless engine . . . on second thoughts I'll pass. I couldn't muster the effort to raise the can so dragged it instead. The metal can scraped across gravel; I hoped nothing sharp would slice through its base, leaving a trail of highly flammable fluid. The things we do in the act of retaliation. As I tugged, the jerry can wedged itself into the rough surface. I squatted into a low stance like a dog taking a dump and strained, lifting it enough to proceed forward.

'You're embarrassing yourself,' said Sammie.

Sammie had observed me every step of the way.

'Have you bought said items?' he asked.

'Indeed I have. Do us a favour, help with this can please?'

'I'm not really dressed for manual labour. But you remind me of a younger version of myself,' he winked, grabbing the jerry can.

Rowdy winds hissed, making squiggly patterns on the canal. Streetlight beams broke through branches. Sam chatted. He was quite an intellectual type, really knowledgeable. He's one of those sorts of people you could speak to forever and amass an extensive understanding of science, politics, nature and life. He explained how electricity works and is generated.

'You're fascinating. How can you remember so much?'

'Before my world turned to turds, I was considered a genius, a marvellous man. I'm able to learn sequences, theories and equations that'd take the average mind days to figure out in hours, sometimes minutes.'

We came off the canal path into a collection of bushes, navigating rabbit holes and cunning foxes.

'Where would you be if you finished your education?'

'As a child I always wanted to design aircrafts. Father took me to airports regularly; we'd watch aeroplanes deploy and retract their wheels on take-off and landing,' he declared fondly.

Incredibly a soaring plane jetted elegantly, carving through clouds into the black blanketing sky.

'Five to twelve, let's hit it,' I said.

Sam paused, peering intently.

'Fokker 100, introduced in 1988 by the Dutch. What a beauty. Only two hundred and eighty-three ever created. Two Rolls-Royce power plants preserved her flight, delivering three hundred jetsetters in comfort. For Christmas, father bought me a replica version. It sat on my windowsill, pride of place. After my horrific schooldays I imagined being a pilot, whisking myself away to a tropical island.'

A dejected Sam dwelled in the silence of what might have been. Without any clear indication, we'd woven a route way below ground. There lived a small circular hut, its straw roof straddling the surrounding ground. Sam broke his quietness.

'Hand me the gear and await the signal,' guided Sam.

'What signal?'

'I'll mention a boy craves a desired result to his quandary. Listen closely.'

I agreed, digging wax out my earhole.

Sam crouched through the door. 'Mrs Doovoo, the lady with a thousand charms.'

'Samuel,' said her eerie voice.

'Call me Sam. Samuel is too formal for colleagues as we are.'

'I concur. Which charm titillates you, Sam?'

Titillates LOL. I waited, growing in apprehension hanging outside the doorway.

'A young boy craves a desired result.'

There's my cue to enter this hut of evilness. I stumbled through the narrow door, grazing my knee.

Mrs Doovoo was a very short and slight lady. Her hut was only four feet high and she still fit comfortably.

'Hello.' I stuck my hand out to humbly greet her.

'Please be seated, gentlemen,' said Mrs Doovoo.

She gave an impression of a woman you wouldn't want to get on the bad side of. We did as told.

'Tell the lady of your complication,' said Sam.

'Well, it all began with a sweet to be known as the Cube over four months ago.'

I rambled for three hours seventeen minutes. Mrs Doovoo huffed in exhaustion at hearing debacle followed by debacle.

'Yikes, Oscar, next time edit the memoirs,' groaned Sam.

Mrs Doovoo's poker face provided no clue if she'd aid me. Her stubborn nose, husky lips and grey eyes seemed painted on.

'The lad is a puny pipsqueak desperately seeking a remedy,' explained Sam.

The teeny tiny woman rubbed a pair of black beads between her fingers. 'Who are the enemies you wish to destroy?'

'Mr Trent, an awful teacher. Classmates Phoebe, Rachael and Mean Dean Jackson. They've made my life a living hell, killing my dog, beating me up and I may be in detention until sixth form.'

Inside the hut the mood intensified. Mrs Doovoo stood up, which in terms of height made no difference. She threw logs onto the fire. I breathed shallowly.

'We've reached an impasse. I can chop down your rivals to ashes. They'll be mere crumbs unable to intimidate or influence others,' she proposed.

'Yes. Squash them. Dismantle their stranglehold on the year 7 students.' A chilling thrill of excitement smothered me in goosebumps.

'Once I have mixed my medicine you must follow through boy, no backsies.'

'Wouldn't dream of it,' I promised.

'For me to disable those vile people tell me a bit about them.'

'Let's see. Mr Trent has a sweat gland problem and stinks out his whole classroom. Phoebe's an artist; she draws exquisite paintings routinely. Rachael's stunning and is obsessed with her image. Dean loves football, that's where his talents lie.'

Mrs Doovoo, who by all accounts was quite striking in the looks department, strapped on a hair net and added ingredients in a miniature cauldron. Large quantities of bones, teeth, a rabbit's foot, fox fur, blue powders, red powders and chillies. To finish the recipe, she spat into the silver bucket. Bales of smoke climbed out the pot; she opened her chimney chute, allowing it to escape. She stirred furiously with a wooden spoon.

The mentioning of my four nemeses sent four feathers on a dreamcatcher shrivelling.

'Invest your courage so I can deliver my client his devious rewards.'

The cauldron's bubbling silenced. A frozen froth wandered out of the lid.

'Now we must chant,' she informed us.

I was specifically instructed to never recite the infamous words in anybody's company. We chanted, holding hands, spinning, jumping and dancing. I felt a bit silly.

'Will the outcome be gruesome?' I asked, sitting back down.

'It all relies on you. I've done my bit.'

'Guide me, oh noble one.'

She searched the cauldron vigorously; her face lit up jubilantly. Mrs Doovoo extracted a leaf, a pair of shoelaces and an extremely fine razor blade.

'We are grateful of your gifts.'

'I'm perplexed, what am I to do with this tat?'

Mrs Doovoo took exception to my question.

'He's a curious young chap,' implied Sam.

The remaining liquid was filtered and a few droplets were secured into a vial.

She fetched a zip-lock bag off her shelf. 'These four items are weapons built to wreak havoc.'

'Show me how.'

'Take this blade and switch it with the one in Phoebe's pencil sharpener. This leaf? Rub it gently on Rachael's make-up equipment, combs, hair bobbles, eyeliner pencils and brushes. See those laces? Let them dry out first, then re-lace Dean's football boots. Drop just a smidge of this vial in Mr Trent's drink, shake it well and enjoy.'

'I like,' I winked.

'Remember the consequences are almost irreversible.'

Tomorrow Oscar Smart rocks Winterberry High to its fragile foundation.

CHAPTER 18

Just Desserts

I achieved a rare feat by being up before mother, only because I never went to sleep. I was as tired as a marathon runner on his or her twenty-fifth mile. I poured myself a mug of coffee. Yuck so . . . so bitter, don't know how adults drink it. I used honey to make the taste bearable. Eager wasn't the word; with Mrs Doovoo's products safely in hand Winterberry High would reap what it had sown.

'Oscar get up, you are not becoming a lazy child,' shouted mom. She awaited my response; silence greeted her.

'Oscar, I won't call you again. I'll be up with a bucket of water.' Mom wandered into the kitchen.

'You're getting quite mean in your advanced age,' I grinned.

Mother was befuddled seeing me beaming at her. I ate a banana, getting one of my five a day.

'Did you wet the bed or something, son?'

'Early bird gets the worm,' I said.

'Backpack, lunch and homework?'

'Done, done and done.'

'Wow! My boy's independent,' she lauded.

Bustling into the kitchen came dad. He made it a personal mission no matter how fatigued he was after work he'd sit and eat breakfast with us.

'I swear blind last night I saw you catching the city bus,' said dad.

He's right. I also spotted his orange car along the route.

'Too young to be sneaking out, son. Going clubbing, were you?'

I laughed unconvincingly. 'Preposterous, father.'

'Funny you say that honey, Marie at number forty-two told me she saw Oscar at the shopping centre yesterday,' said mom.

Had I been rumbled? Change topic immediately.

'What's the weather saying today?' I asked.

'Rain, rain same old really,' replied mom.

'Darling, you haven't seen my driving license? It's always in my wallet.'

'Sorry.'

'It'll be in the last place you look, dad.'

'Meaning what exactly?' investigated dad.

I flustered. 'Just a general saying. It'll turn up somewhere.'

Dad tightened his bathrobe. 'Okay. For a second there I thought you knew something. Perhaps you borrowed my license to buy booze.'

How could he know?

I erupted into a fit of laughter.

Dad frowned highly concerned. 'Where is the joke?'

'I'm imagining myself trying to buy illegal goods from an off license or petrol station.'

Dad sniggered. 'You're a good son, one to be trusted.'

By the skin of my teeth I swerved his accusations and skipped on to school.

I pencilled Phoebe in first to sharpen my tools. Get it? We had art from ten till eleven. My operation needed patience, craft and subtlety. Phoebe protected her expensive material like soldiers would a king. No lending. No touching. Fortunately for me, we were using a multitude of watercolours. Set in the middle of each table was a rinsing bucket, which Phoebe hogged. Fine by me.

'You'll have to find elsewhere to clean your pathetic bushes,' barked Phoebe.

'Miss said we have to share.'

'You'll corrupt the water.'

When I went to swill my brush off, she wrenched the pot back. I leaned further over the table. Phoebe dragged the canister closer to her.

One monster nudge from me and a splattering of water made contact with her skirt.

'Oscar you pillock!' she screamed.

'I'm a clumsy sod. Accept my apology.'

Our art teacher viewed the mess. 'Phoebe, you go to the bathroom and clean yourself up. I'll find a skirt from lost and found. I'll be back in five minutes, class. No fighting, biting or vandalising property.'

No one took a blind bit of notice. With both teacher and Phoebe absent I went to work. I clipped off the plastic pencil shaving holder to get to blade. Classroom order had broken down into straight chaos. Boys filled balloons with metallic paints – a handful of teacher's cars were sure to be defaced. I used a mini screwdriver leftover from my remote-control robot tools. The flat head screwdriver hooked up perfectly. Like a tyre change in a pit stop, I extracted her original blade, slotting in my new and improved version. I fastened the plastic holder and resumed painting.

Phoebe down. I needn't gloat. Mr Trent was second on the checklist and, all things said, my most troublesome foe. He ate his disgusting sandwiches in the teachers' lounge, which I had no real reason to enter. But on this day I saw the sweet, happy and helpful figure of Miss Louise foxtrot inside. She never walked anywhere, consistently practicing dance steps. I kept the vial in my trouser pocket for easy usage. I swiftly knocked on the door and took my mind to the saddest place possible, witnessing little Einstein's crumpled up paw.

'All right, chick,' said Miss Louise.

'I'm fed up,' I whined.

'What's up, cupcake?'

Miss Louise wasn't a typical teacher, a very quirky person in Winterberry terms. She had pet names for everyone you were a cupcake, chick or buttercup.

'I feel lost without being in drama club.'

I'd been excluded from performing arts lessons after Rachael argued she couldn't work like this; regular diva behaviour.

'Come in,' she tenderly invited.

For all Winterberry High's design flaws, the teachers' lounge felt like it had been ripped from a luxurious homes website. Shoes were taken off at the door. Foamy shaggy carpets massaged the soles of your feet. Each had separate colours – red, yellow, pink and green – they sort of ease your burden upon entry. For fun and entertainment snooker tables, dart boards and air hockey. I sat on their super-duper settee and the spongy cushion caressed my bottom.

'I loved having a male cast member. It brought a variety to my production.'

In truth, I could take or leave acting. 'The stage, thousands of eyes all compelled by my wonderful flair,' I fibbed.

She jumped out of her seat as if someone pushed the ejector button. 'The heart wants what the heart wants. You should do a solo act on stage for all the parents.'

'I don't know about that,' I feared.

'Dream the dream. I see it in my vision – hundreds of stubborn parents being soothed by your expert skills.'

Her enthusiasm overwhelmed me.

'Let's sleep on it,' I proposed.

'Sleep is for the dead. I'm alive with creative sparks igniting me to produce a masterpiece,' Miss Louise closed her eyes, visualising her perfect play.

When opportunity knocks you have to answer. Miss Louise waltzed into her daydream blind, deaf and out of breath. I ransacked the teachers' fridge lunchbox by lunchbox. To my delight, on the second shelf on the right in cap letters, I saw MR TRENT'S HANDS OFF. I quickly glanced over my shoulder.

Peeling off the lid his decomposing ingredients burnt my nose hairs. I tugged off the sports cap, tipping the whole vial in, even though Mrs Doovoo said a small droplet could gain the desired effect. While Mr Trent can choose whenever to swallow his medicine, I exited the teachers' lounge before Miss Louise realised.

I surveyed how to tie Dean down. Winterberry High's year 7 boys had a top of the table clash against Moss Town after school. Here's my theory. Somehow, I had got to exchange laces unsuspected. However, our school team leave last lesson early. As the squad promptly laboured off to prepare, I waved for the teacher's awareness.

She finally made eye contact. 'Yes, Oscar?'

'May I go to the toilet?'

She flicked her wrist watch. 'Hold it in for ten minutes.'

'I've got a weak bladder, miss, it's urgent.' My voice included that sudden emergency pitch.

'Very well.'

I sprinted down the corridor. Mr Russell headed in the opposite direction.

'Walk, don't run,' he demanded.

At breakneck speed I blitzed floors one and two, perching myself near the boys' changing room. The lads were in high spirits, rowdy about the big game. A win today puts them six points clear with a superior goal difference. Dean arrived fashionably late, his goons carrying his boot bag.

Once the last guy turned up, phase two went into motion.

Ring! Ring! Ring! I pressed the fire alarm.

'Keep it moving people, to the fire assembly point. It's only a drill,' organised the teachers.

The half-dressed football squad rushed out in their boxer shorts. Boys' locker rooms can be a ghastly place: sweat, body odour, blood, snot and spit are all elements. Dean's equipment stood out; his initials were stitched into his shorts, socks and football boots. He wore a fantastic pair of wafer-light golden boots. I studied how his laces were strapped up. Soon as I felt confident enough, I hauled out his original laces and criss-crossed my remodelled addition.

Three out of four in one day wasn't bad going. Rachael could wait for a later date. I'm beat. Plus, Dean is about to display his new footballing skills.

CHAPTER 19

Karma

Echoes of joy and excitement greeted Dean as his twinkle toes contacted the pitch.

'Deano! Deano! here we go,' screamed the adoring Phoebe.

Moss Town made Winterberry High look like angels. These hunched grizzly apes trudge onto the field brawling for conflict. They'd dominated every opponent and gathered notoriety for their smash mouth style of play.

'Are they supposed to be in our year?' I asked Lance.

'Moss Town's children grow differently.'

Dean was considered a gifted athlete; fifteen goals in nine games proved it. He received man of the match awards and the captain's armband for his trouble. But Moss Town's counterpart overshadowed his solid frame. They came to the centre circle and shook hands professionally. Moss Town won the coin toss and decided to kick off.

The ref blew his whistle. Moss Town kicked from left to right in their all white away kit.

It was a tepid affair in the early going, no real chances. The defenders kept a high line.

'Get it to Dean,' yelled his parents.

The Winterberry goalkeeper caught an easy cross and released it to Dean on the left flank. The crowd responded in elated glee. Dean eyed the first defender. He shimmied left only to jink right. His opposing player didn't buy the dummy, nicking the ball and starting another attack.

'Shake it off, Dean,' barked his parents.

Moss Town pressured Winterberry and, without Dean as an outlet, they were pinned in their own box. The deadlock was broken from a corner kick; a floated cross sailed over the at-sea keeper. Dean timed his jump incorrectly, heading into his own net.

'Wicked!' I cheered.

'It's an own goal, der-brain,' said Lance.

Dean stunk horribly. Routine passes missed targets. He consistently got tackled and injured his own players.

'What you doing lad?' asked coaches and fans.

Dean shrugged, miffed, baffled and totally confused.

Mrs Doovoo's goodies rewarded me in euphoria.

In thirty-five minutes of play Dean racked up two own goals, fluffed a shot in front of a gaping goal and blazed a penalty high, wide and anything but handsome. He also collected a straight red card for diving. Tremendous! Needless to say, Winterberry lost, getting hammered four nil.

Dean failed miserably. Good. And on to the next one.

Rachael's lead act in Miss Louise's adapted version of Romeo and Juliet gets underway tonight. With me being a respectable piano player Rachael's solo act would now have a cameo from yours truly. Brilliant; this gave me ample time to inflict her suffering. I rubbed, wiped and smeared the coarse leaf over her foundation, blusher, primer, combs and hairbrush. After her costume fitting, she returned, attracting gasps from other theatre students.

'Take a picture, it'll last longer,' she flaunted.

Rachael's presence brought Miss Louise to tears. 'You're gonna steal the show.'

If you only knew, Miss Louise. If only.

'The Haunted One! Get out,' ordered Rachael, linking a Tudor-style pendant around her neck.

'I'll be limbering up in the hall.'

'No one cares, boy.'

'Be pleasant Rachael, you two are partners,' explained Miss Louise.

'He's my underling, a puppet to the puppet master.'

Her abusive comments made her impending fall from grace all the sweeter.

I whirled into main hall. Its capacity was six hundred, but extra seats had been added for this eventful performance.

'Oscar, big hug and kisses!' eagerly hollered mother.

Rachael giggled behind the curtain at me. But he who laughs last laughs longest. Sitting on the piano stool, I glided my fingers across the Baby Grand. She purred fantastically. Every key erupted in sound. The spotlight dimmed as the red curtains floated away. Rachael glowed, dressed to the nines in a corset, overflowing gown and shinning headdress. Disappointingly her skin was unblemished. It had me wondering if Mrs Doovoo had been all smoke and no fire. We began the piece with a little intro. I stroked the keys and she skipped to my loo. Now who's the puppet master? Dance step upon dance step Rachael's makeup cracked, crumbling to reveal pimples and rashes. They developed from forehead to chin. As for her shair, the renowned locks shredded quicker than a moulting cat.

Parents' eyes bulged in disbelief.

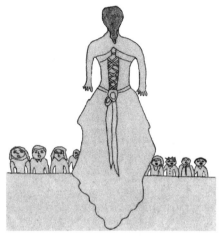

Miss Louise fluttered, disturbed. 'Kill the lights. Draw the curtains. Oscar, play us out.'

I serenaded the audience with a catalogue of songs.

'That's my boy,' I heard mother rejoicing.

Backstage Rachael scrubbed her face raw with soap. But the more she cleansed the more complimentary blotches formed.

'Could it be chickenpox?' asked Miss Louise.

'No, I had it at seven,' sighed Rachael. 'It's getting worse. I'm hideous.'

'Those awful teenage years, your hormones are discombobulated.'

'But Miss Louise, I can't live being ugly.'

Miss Louise loosened her string corset, although Rachael's face stayed red. There's such potency in Mrs Doovoo's epic brew.

'Beauty isn't skin deep; it's what's on the inside that counts,' preached Miss.

Bad luck Rachael is rotten to the bone.

Between Dean's mishaps and Rachael's facial I became delirious. Amazed parents left the hall speechless; words that were spoken were redundant.

'Did you see her face?'

'What happened to the girl? It's astonishing.'

'My kid is the best piano player in the country,' endlessly bragged mom.

I ticked two names off my enemies list.

Phoebe, you're the central character, so come on down and receive your grand prize.

By now, we all accept Phoebe can draw, paint, shade and colour, –whoop dee doo. Her unique abilities had taken her a step further than A* status. She'd reached the national finals, where her work, among five other hopefuls, was to be displayed in the local art gallery for high-profile judges. Success here would put her firmly on the map to superstardom – not if I had anything to say about it.

Golly. Do I sound vindictive?

The gallery paraded marvellous artistic sculptures and casts to very extreme and outright dangerous statues.

Everything had a polished, snobby mood. I loved it. Wealthy people ate vol-au-vents and elegantly sipped cocktails in black bow ties. Males greeted males kissing on both cheeks. Honey I'm home, back where l belong, I thought.

'Oscar, look at this pic,' Lance said amusingly.

'Quit man, Phoebe is gonna unveil her painting any moment.'

Lance got in my face, annoying the bejesus out of me. 'You'll regret it.'

'Fine, if it'll stop you spitting on me.'

He walked rapidly over to a six-foot canvas, nervously excited. What had him so intoxicated?

Fifty-seven minutes later we remained ogling the photo.

'Perverts,' shouted Phoebe.

'Our final competitor is Phoebe, from Winterberry High,' said a committee member.

Rapturous applause, claps, stomps and cheers raised the roof. Commoners! Can't take them anywhere.

'Guys and girls, I'd like to present my painting to you, I call it "a part of me"' Phoebe said with teary eyes.

Her father rubbed her arm tenderly. 'Go for it love.'

An emotional Phoebe lingered a sec before slipping off the cover.

'What's it supposed to be?' pondered a judge.

Colours came off dull and overlapped. The paint flaked, eating through parts of canvas.

A despondent, ashamed and broken-hearted Phoebe placed dead last.

'How could this be?' she bawled.

What goes around comes around.

I'm three goals to the good. Mr Trent would signal a home run. If you recall Mr Trent organised my hundred hours of detention. He made it his personal mission to see I sat every pigging minute. He routinely escorted me to detention, but of late lacked the same enthusiasm. In Geography lessons sweat gathered as before – in fact more so, except now only oozing out aromas like vanilla, blueberries and mangos. His taste buds were shot too. It got to a point where Mr Trent regularly visited his G.P, taking all kinds of medicine attempting to regain his quirky taste in food. Poor old sod.

CHAPTER 20

Pop Quiz

Karma is a switch – at least I think that's the saying. I owned Winterberry High; my power play made me feared. Children pleaded to do my homework. Teachers allowed me to play darts in their swanky lounge any time I pleased. And the girls threw themselves at me. I had to beat them off with a stick. If you believe that then I've got a glass hammer and rubber screws to sell you.

Nevertheless, a power dimension had shifted. Dean, Phoebe and Rachael's reign on top was short-lived. One hit wonders. Other than their single qualities they brought nothing of substance. Mr Trent was on leave, for stress supposedly. But I knew better. Miss Louise explained he'd booked himself in for an experimental procedure to unblock his sinuses. Substitute teachers are fabulous; they never understand the subject so running amok is easy. Today Mr Russell was our alternative. You'll see as you get older that when you are in the company of superiors, maybe a boss, supervisor, manager and hopefully not judge or jury, automatically our demeanours differ. We'll sit up straight, pencil, pen, ruler and exercise book open to a blank page. Even the most mischievous kids expressed an eagerness for knowledge. We all anticipated Mr Russell telling us to copy out of a text book.

'Relax children, I'm not a goggle-eyed monster like Mr Trent,' he smiled.

Every boy and girl unravelled, their tense posture slithering back to our frumpy position.

'Exercise books away kids. Today we're having a surprise pop quiz on general issues.' Mr Russell declared. 'Split into group of six groups of five.'

Cliques and crews formally combined; geeks on one table, jocks to another. The glamour girls sat centrally, as the world revolves around them, the oddball kids took a table near the front and the foreign exchange students stuck together too. Five out of six groups were formed. It only left a batch of fascinating characters me, Lance, also Dean, whose posse had rebranded, Rachael, or as she's better known porridge face due to her skin texture, and the once-great artist Phoebe. Teacher's pet Stefan left a sheet of A4 paper on each desk.

'Right teams, you're gonna need a name. Please give yourself a name in bold letters. No rudeness, Ben Dover or Amanda Hugginkiss aren't acceptable,' explained Mr Russell.

The trio of misfits stared at Lance and I worried.

'Boo,' whispered Lance.

All three jumped out of their shoes, terrified.

'We are called Lance and Oscar's Little Helpers,' I announced.

'Whatever you decide is all right by us,' squeaked Dean.

Rachael and Phoebe instantly agreed.

'This is what it's come down to,' mumbled Phoebe, breaking her fifth pencil on her sketch board. 'Again!' she complained.

'Ease up with the pressure; let the lead breathe,' said Rachael, cracking her tenth mirror in the last hour.

Mu ha ha ha mu ha ha ha! Mu ha ha ha mu ha ha ha! Mu ha ha ha mu ha ha ha!

Lance nudged me with his elbow. 'Why are you laughing so loud?'

'I'm encouraged. We'll snatch victory from our competitors,' I boasted.

'How? We've got three flops to contend with,' he boldly pointed to the confidence-drained teammates.

'Seriously, we'll stay out of harm's way,' spoke Dean softly. His old gang threw rubbers at his head. Dean never reacted. In fact, he politely picked them up, returning them back.

'Good little helpers,' winked Lance.

'Question one, when was the Battle of Hastings?'

Being an astute historian I scribbled down October 14th 1066.

'Question two. In which year did Fokker put the 100 into production?'

Beautiful; twenty-nine pupils scratched heads, pulled hair and bit fingers.

'Who knows that sort of stuff?' said a bamboozled Lance.

God bless you Sam. I wrote 1988.

Over the course of the quiz the questions grew more difficult. Tables fought, floundering for constructive answers. People panted, losing their senses.

'What's two add two?' grunted one kid.

'If I travel at thirty mph (the speed limit in built-up areas) how long will it take to go sixty miles?' panicked the geek table.

Winning seemed certain. Mr Russell concluded his entertaining quiz with a couple of questions I was unfamiliar with.

'Question eighteen. Who is the Premiership all-time record goal scorer? And for a bonus point how many goals did he score?'

Only footballer I know is Gary Lineker from his crisp adverts. One wrong answer will just cut into the winning border. I left it blank. Dean's eyes lit up alarmingly, but he didn't have the assurance anymore.

'Dean, you must. With an encyclopedic footballing brain,' I said, gently coaxing him out his shell.

He anxiously played with his shoelaces, then, quiet as a baby mouse. 'Alan Shearer, 260 goals.'

'Good on you Dean,' I praised.

'This is for the artists out there. Who painted Bedroom in Arles? An extra point goes to whoever can tell me the actual size of the picture.'

You're jogging me. What fanatical artist would be capable of such information? A girl who never leaves home without a graphite pencil is who.

'Phoebs, lay it on me.'

She shrugged, reluctant to inform us, 'I'm unsure of everything. What I once felt was true now showers me in lies.'

'Buried internally is your artistic nature. Unleash it,' I motivated.

'Vincent van Gogh, seventy-two by ninety centimetres,' she replied.

'Incredible,' screamed Lance.

'Question twenty. I'm a French retail clothing company established in 1854. Who am I?'

Oh, you dirty rascal. Someone must be engrossed in fashion. Luckily, I've got that sort of girl at my disposal.

'Rachael, shoot,' I said, making eye contact, the first person to do so since her facial demise.

She took no real persuading.

'Louis Vuitton,' Rachael confirmed.

'Well done, Rach.'

'Lucky guess,' she said, taking clumps of hair to the bin.

'Pencils down, class,' instructed Mr Russell.

Top boy Stefan collected up our papers. Mr Russell marked each sheet to tally the scores. Dean, Rachael and Phoebe held gormless poses, their heads hung like clock pendulums. Usually schoolwork wasn't of importance to these popular kids. However they were all hot under the collar.

'How do you think we did?' wondered Lance.

'Never in doubt. Those three answers our little helpers gave us completed our championship form,' I responded.

Mr Russell ruffled the sheets, increasing the suspense.

'I can't take another loss,' grumbled Phoebe.

'I've forgot the winning feeling,' said Dean. Coach removed his captaincy for lacking a positive influence on players.

'The fifth winners are Glamour Girls, ran close by Exchange for Change, third but first on the podium Buck Nakad.'

It couldn't be helped; we chuckled, amused.

'Excellent, boys,' Mr Russell was fair yet strict. 'So, you five idiots have volunteered to clean chewing from underneath each table.'

'Mr Russell, what wrong with a little light-hearted comedy?' protested the group.

'At whose expense?' he flipped over the tables; there dried bubble gum covered the metal frame.

To say Winterberry's equipment was outdated is like saying the sun's hot and water's wet. Etched in the wooden table someone proclaimed, "Backstreet Boys Rock".

Who are the Backstreet Boys when they're at home?

As the immature lads chipped away, Mr Russell released winners one and two.

'Two groups one spot. $E=mc^2$ take on Lance and Oscar's Little Helpers.'

Sweat built above Rachael's brow; it made its way around zits, navigated pimples, ploughed over spots and slid down blackheads. Life's full of lumps and bumps.

Oscar, you wicked person.

'Pop Quiz Kings and Queens are . . . '

$E=mc^2$ frowned; a team of pure males wouldn't have queens.

'Lance and Oscar's Little Helpers.'

The leader of the geek squad tipped his head in a way to congratulate us.

'Stick it, losers. The brains trust? Please. More like brains rust. Loooooser!' I shaped my hand to make a giant L.

'Academic achievers, let's crack the books.'

One can only admire their hunger for new teachings.

'There's a lot to be said for a man who is tactful in success,' said Mr Russell; pulling out a black sack he jiggled, shaking it. I heard the plastic packets rumbling.

'Who won?' inquired Rachael, combing out her split ends.

'Lance and I carried us over the threshold.'

Mr Russell stood over my shoulder in a hard-nose stance, arms crossed. He was a gangly man with his peanut head and stubby moustache which looked like a dominant slug nestled above the upper lip. Many good guys have moustaches, for instance Adolf Hitler and Saddam Hussein. Sorry, I said good guys 'It's a team effort; one hand washes the other.'

'Yes sir, no I in team,' I agreed.

'Isn't there?' asked one of Dean's old cronies.

Mr Russell almost resigned where he stood. 'God help us.'

Overall those guys were never able-minded. Dean spoke and they followed. It's what prevented them from charging towards oncoming traffic, eating paste or downing bleach. Without his steady hand at the wheel one dum-dum dared another to taste a urinal cake. DON'T TRY THIS AT HOME.

'Winning unit, pick one item from my sack.'

'My sack,' the Buck Nakad leader joked, flicking chewing gum into the air.

'Heads,' said his buddy, knocking it onto the bin lid.

'You're supposed to be young adults,' groaned Mr Russell.

'Some of these kids could do with being left back a year or two, sir,' I commented.

'Additional years would put me in an early grave.'

Lance, weedy but greedy, rummaged through Mr Russell's bag. He searched low and high.

'Now or never son,' hurried Mr Russell.

Lance gingerly plucked out a gobstopper. 'A do over please, I hate gobstoppers.'

'No can do. Oscar, make it snappy.'

I grabbed the shiniest packet available. I'm a pro after all. It felt familiar, like wearing an old pair of trainers. As my hand surfaced out the bag a vile foe presented itself in his mega mix. Mr Sugar's smirking exterior logo embroiled my anger. Nation of Sugar's truly incredible resurgence hurt father and me. He'd weathered Candy Planet's storm to once again cause more fillings than potholes. Inflamed, I hastily tore the packaging to itsy-bitsy pieces cola bottles, gummy bears and strawberries scattered.

Desperate kids scavenged sweets off the dirty floor. Rats had more dignity.

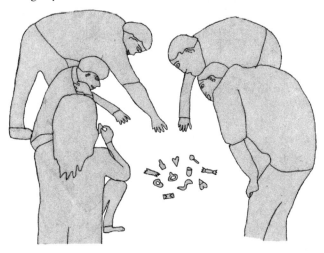

CHAPTER 21

Keep Your Enemies Closer

Up until Mr Sugar's sighting, today would've been deemed a roaring success. Not a punch, kick, scrap or claw was inflicted. Hell, I cracked a feeble smile at eleven twenty. Damagingly, I fled home seething. Mr Sugar got away scot-free.

How long will it take to build a confectionery empire to rival and eventual outsell his? I detailed a time frame of my monstrous upswing to his collapse; rounded down perhaps twenty-five years. Supper tasted bitter, not just because mother measured out too many gravy granules. Being spiteful can consume your everyday activities, providing you with constant rage.

'How was school? Have you established yourself as a firm favourite?' asked mom.

'It's as expected,' I grunted aggressively.

'Check your attitude at the door, mighty man.'

'Whatevs.'

'That's not my son. He's a loveable guy.' She didn't ask for nor deserve my ignorant behaviour.

'Soz, school work, gotta get those good grades,' I explained.

Mom scrunched up her eyes. She dropped her knife and fork, sliding her chair next to mine. 'Look, big school's challenging.

Inside you're probably experiencing some physical differences. Shall we go in the lounge and chat?'

'Why can't we talk in here?'

Mom came across skittish. 'I got an educational video.'

I'm baffled.

Dad covered his face, abashed.

'What sort of video?'

'About,' she paused, mortified.

'Oh, my days, spit it out woman,' said dad agitatedly.

Ding dong!

'The birds and the Bees! You're far too old to believe babies come from storks.'

'I'll get it.' My mind reached the door at *dong*.

'Conversation isn't done with, son.'

'Smooth. Real smooth,' huffed dad.

'Exactly. He needs a man to discuss his personal growth spurt, among other things. Can you ask your brother or dad to have a word?'

Dad tried to apply his fierce stare; hard to accomplish when filing your nails. He ceased cutting out an article on beauty tips. 'I'm a twenty-first century man, not afraid to admit to a sensitive side.'

Ding dong!

'Coming,' I yelled.

'All right, is your bra on too tight?' Mom sniggered, clearing the table.

'How very dare you?' Dad's tone wavered, upset.

'Sorry, you're a delicate flower.'

Father's watch bleeped, meaning his conditioner had to be rinsed. He reflected on the argument. Determining his example of manliness wasn't accurate.

'Boys go through a process named . . .' Dad stalled, unsure of the precise medical term.

'Puberty. It generally starts around eleven years old for boys and ten for girls,' I responded.

PUBERTY

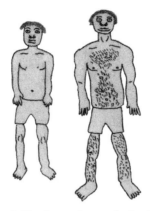

'Glad that's sorted. During puberty the body produces . . .' He scrolled his apps, games, viral videos, shopping, banking and betting, along with a thousand others, but not one on the human body.

'We produce testosterone.'

'And testosterone is?' Dad enquired in a mystified manner. I gathered he knew less than I did.

'Testosterone is a steroid.'

'No steroids in this household.'

'It's a steroid hormone we manufacture normally.'

Mom stopped cleaning the table and sat down, enchanted by my vast awareness of biology. 'Is it just a human practice?'

'Mammals, reptiles, birds . . . in fact a majority of species,' I answered.

Mama and papa were blown away.

'Oscar's got a magnificent grasp on human chemistry,' admired dad.

Ding dong!

'On my way; you taught me it's rude to keep a visitor waiting.'

Whoever's knocking I love you. I unhooked the latch, twisted the key, unlocked the three deadbolts and removed the chain. No such thing as too careful in Winterberry. I was taken aback; Phoebe stood on my doorstep.

'Fancy hanging out?'

Uncertain of her agenda, but fearing mother would have follow-up questions, I jumped at the chance to escape.

'Mom, I'm off out.'

She rushed into the living area, up to her elbows in soap suds. 'I wasn't finished.'

Now Phoebe couldn't draw worth a lick. That being said, she still maintained her fantastic looks. This bothered mother extremely.

'Who's your lady friend?'

'I'm Phoebe. Nice to meet you, Mrs Smart,' she said super politely.

'Honey, get in here right away,' screamed my mom.

Dad wandered into view; his hair conditioner had crusted over.

'Oscar's dossing with this young girl. Got anything to say?'

Dad picked at his frosted quiff. 'Have a splendid time. Don't do anything I wouldn't do.'

I slammed the door behind me, shifting down the driveway. Mom peeked through the curtains. Their elevated voices rang out.

'Good on you, Oscar,' beamed dad.

'I'm too young to be a grandparent,' she wailed.

Phoebe and I exited Winterberry Road in deathly silence. I get tongue-tied speaking to girls. It was a cloudy day; from time to time the sun poked its head out, as if playing a game of peek-a-boo.

'Painting much?' I said curiously.

'I dabble occasionally.' A great level of sorrow was displayed in her body language. She flopped, changing direction with how the wind blew.

'Keep plugging away, girlie,' I inspired.

'I do. Dad bought me a completely new pencil set.'

I gulped, disheartened. 'Even a pencil sharpener?'

'Yes, the lot,' she replied. 'Look. Disaster accompanied by disaster,' she whined.

Her drawing pad was littered in diabolical creations, horse-frogs and sheep-cats.

Dean had entered the picture; he prowled the street kicking a ball. His skills were so eroded he spent more time fishing it from underneath cars.

'Hello, Oscar,' greeted Dean.

This is a trap – they're gonna do something horrific.

'We've been sworn enemies for months. Why you being so nice?' I asked.

Dean seemed timid. He mumbled. 'I'm a new person. Less mean. Make peace not war, dude.'

'Really?'

'Honest as the day is long.'

'We all realised, do bad to others and you'll pay in your own way,' said Phoebe.

Wow, it takes a lot to apologise.

'Rachael feels utterly terrible too. Unfortunately, she won't leave her house,' said Dean.

'Succeeding in that pop quiz earlier gave us a beacon of hope,' added Phoebe.

Dean and Phoebe were being genuine. We chatted for a while. Lance had recently begun participating in an art program at the local college, on the off chance he'd see real life women. So, hanging with kids my own age felt surreal. I demonstrated my robot's array of abilities. They were awestruck.

'Sick, Oscar,' they exclaimed.

Dean called for me daily with his posse out of commission. He cut a lonely figure kicking the ball against neighbours' walls.

'That boy is outside again, Oscar. What a depressed kid, so gloomy. Thankfully you're his mate,' mom said fondly.

Experiencing Dean's torment frequently crushed my joy.

'I work with what I'm given.'

'Modest, humble and compassionate; a son a mother will always adore,' she squeezed me, but as we embraced a pain built inside the pit of my stomach.

'Dean. What you up to?'

He halted kicking the ball. 'I'm going fishing this weekend. Dad said I could invite one person. How would you like to go?'

Fishing. This is it. His masterstroke. Take me out on a boat so I can sleep with the fishes.

'Sure, why not?' I accepted.

CHAPTER 22

Catch of the Day

In a span of three weeks Dean and I went from battering seven bells out of one another to having a slumber party. What gives? The Jackson family were awfully gracious. They catered to my every need; his mother made dinner, being wary of my spicy food problem. The Jackson family tree consisted of seven: mom and dad, no surprise there, Dean and four older sisters. I must be important; they were eating off proper plates instead of the paper ones I saw stacked up in bulk in their pantry. Nonetheless, dinner was served, a British favourite – Toad in the hole with creamy mash potatoes and Brussels sprouts. Sprouts. If I ever meet the putrid human who engaged in consuming this baby cabbage, he'd regret it.

'Everything satisfactory, Oscar?' eagerly asked his mom.

The Yorkshire pudding was crisp and bubbly. The sausages tasted sensational. Sausages are the best part of the pig, you know. Pig's ears, snout, belly, bones and tail all grounded up to a mushy consistency then gloriously cased in intestines. Anybody for hot dogs?

'Absolutely, right on the money,' I said.

'Are you sure there's nothing else I could get you?'

'I don't mean to be a pain, but could I bother you for some salt?'

Like a bat out of hell she zoomed into the kitchen, opening cabinets. 'Hubby, I can't see it. You'll have to go to the supermarket.'

'It's a non-issue. I'll go without,' I stressed.

'A guest of Dean won't suffer a meal absent of salt,' she implied.

'We'll be two minutes. Mary, you're in charge,' informed Dean's dad.

'Oscar, would you like anything specific while we're out?' pleasantly said Dean's mother.

'Don't go out on my account.'

'Any friend of Dean is a friend of ours,' she replied, taking hers and her husband's dinners and shoving them in the oven.

What are they doing to me? So warm-hearted, kind-spirited and accommodating, with Dean's parents buying a massive variety y of salts. I mean Rock salt, Sea salt, Table salt and weirdly Bath salts. His crafty older sisters piled their Brussels sprouts onto Dean's plate.

'No way, you remember last time,' he complained.

'So? Diarrhoea won't kill you,' vented his oldest sister.

'Actually, diarrhoea has killed thousands globally,' I stated.

His four siblings swivelled. A frightening intent glowed from their faces. They snatched my plate, placing an equal amount of sprouts to Dean's.

'We have our very own eating contest,' beamed his sister, bringing out a stopwatch.

'You can't. See, this is why no one likes us,' said Dean.

The green veg smelled ghastlier than I recalled.

'Gobble them up or else,' she threatened.

'Or else what will happen?' I stupidly asked.

The four sturdy girls stood by our sides. Each licked their index finger. They used one arm to hold us to our seats.

'Ready, girls?'

Dean squirmed and squealed. 'I'll eat the lot, no qualms.'

'Ditto.'

'Too late, wet willy time.'

Their slimy fingers slipped into my earholes. They twisted, poked, prodded and drilled. I winced, disgusted. The warm spit collected on my lobe. Sludge! Cotton buds never reached these depths. At one point I'm sure their fingers touched in the middle.

'Ladies, withdraw. You may continue to eat.'

Dean and I scoffed soggy, dreadful and lukewarm sprouts. Dean squeezed the juice out the veg; this meant he could load more on board. I played it safe with a bite, chomp, chew and swallow technique. After several minutes of eating my jaw ached but at least the ordeal was over.

'Tomorrow's gonna be an early start. Let me tell you, Oscar, you haven't fished until you hit the North Sea,' bragged Jimmy, Dean's dad.

Before bed, I scrubbed sprout residue out of my teeth and looked online for an ear transplant. I took Dean's bed while he slept on an inflatable mattress. Beneath his bed he owned a rare stash of marvellous comic books. We communicated throughout the night, debating who made a better villain, the Joker or Lex Luthor. And the granddaddy of all questions: Superman v Batman, who wins?

Without a word to the wise morning stole the scene from night. By seven o'clock we were at the fishing yard. Jimmy hired a medium sized boat. Its animated engine vibrated, frothing in the water. Off we sailed, surging into a navy-blue setting. The ride was choppy; waves thumped our boat. The sea seemed angry and bitter towards me, discharging saltwater into my face. Was nature sending me a message?

Dean unpacked endless equipment: hooks, reels, rods, bait and nets. We had coasted to the flat bang centre of nowhere. The North Sea ran deep. Gazing out, I couldn't gauge where the sky ended and the sea began. Jimmy shut off the engine as we floated. Dean still struggled untangling his reel wire.

'You're not sea sick, are you?' asked Jimmy.

'No, I feel free as butterfly shedding its cocoon,' I replied.

Dean had ultimately got his wires crossed and the reel coiled around his arm. Jimmy observed, rather annoyed. 'Secure the reel to rod first, then thread the line. How my times do I have to explain?'

'I'm on it, dad. Don't mind me.' Dean wrestled and tussled, readdressing his rod.

'The lad has been good for nothing lately. Fallen down the pecking order with his football coaches, fake friends disappeared . . . only the true ones stand by you.' Jimmy rubbed my head.

My burning feeling of remorse kept rising up.

'Fortunes will surely flip,' I said, knowing I was the culprit.

'Dean's rugged personality gives off this hard image. At home he's a pussycat, with four unruly sisters constantly pestering him. They gang up on the poor boy. If he dares tattle those girls serve discipline swiftly.'

I saw a sincere look of concern in Jimmy. He whispered so Dean couldn't overhear.

'He doesn't allow me to tell people this. However, Oscar, you've got a trustworthy face. Last week scouts terminated his trial at United's academy. He was inconsolable. Threw his football boots away and promised never to play again.'

'Footballers go through dry spells,' I explained under pressure.

'Not him. Some humans are born to do certain things. Roald Dahl with writing, Michael Schumacher with driving, Tiger Woods and golf. Deano was given brown eyes, black hair and an eye for goal to compete with any modern-day icon. Cristiano Ronaldo,

Dean belongs in that category. A prolific goal scoring machine. Now he can't hit a barn door with a banjo.'

What has become of me? I've converted into the one thing I despise: a bully. To top it off, I go and befriend his likeable family. Shame on you, Oscar.

The ocean remained bumpy. Still we hooked fish bait to our rods and cast them overboard.

'Father, son and Oscar fly fishing off the North Sea. A day to be immortalised,' cheered his dad.

Dean's response was mute, as was mine.

'Fishing is a wonderful hobby. We're using replica fish to tempt the big brutes onto our lines. Kids, wiggle your rods.'

I jiggled the rod slightly; only slightly. Oddly enough my line shook furiously. It bent. Whatever tugged away wasn't shy.

I gripped my rod tightly. Animal against human. Let's do this.

'Hold him, Oscar,' ordered Jimmy.

'He's too strong.' I leant back, straining.

'Unreel about a foot of line.'

Dean watched on excitedly.

'Won't I lose him?'

'No, he'll attempt to gain better purchase. You'll sense a good yank.'

I gave the line some slack and so it unfolded little fishy took the bait. He clamped on full force.

'Now seal the deal,' said Jimmy.

Dean prepared a net to scoop up our catch of the day.

'Reel! Reel! Reel!' screamed Jimmy.

I fought incredibly hard to retrieve the fish. Credit where credit's due, it battled to the death. Eventually I won out, heaving my prize up off the seabed. Dean netted him delightedly.

'Terrific, Oscar,' he grinned.

Every word of praise I falsely accepted.

'Magnificent Bass there, let see what she weighs,' Jimmy fetched a scale.

Keeping it wrapped in a sling, we weighed the monster. Its enormous size stretched the netting.

'Forty-one pounds! Absolutely brilliant. Quick snap before we toss her back,' Jimmy brought out this funny-looking camera. Said something about winding the film on. A camera that takes film, really?

Dean and me held its scaly skin head to tail.

'Say Bass.'

'Bass,' we replied.

Oscar Smart, you make me sick. I slowly released the fish home and we headed back too.

We sat on deck while Jimmy breezed along the surface.

'How do you like fishing?' Dean asked.

'It's wicked,' I buzzed.

'I know, right? Thinking about becoming a fisherman since this football thing went kaput.'

'Won't Phoebe have to agree?'

'Phoebe's lost her passion for life after her painting debacle.'

'She'll find another creative field,' I said.

156

'Listen, she'd kill me for saying this, but her deceased mother was a painter. Europe's elite portrait artist. Without that connection Phoebe is all at sea.'

'Oh yeah?'

'Remember the gallery project "a part of me"?' Dean said, getting rather emotional.

'How can I forget?'

'It was in remembrance of her mother,' cried Dean. 'No one knows except us.'

The sun waned, on its decline spreading a glowing orange haze.

'What a terrible shame.'

'Rachael got the raw deal. With mine and Phoebe's dilemma we can simply not engage in the activities. Sadly, Rachael's a performer for the church choir.'

Information overload. Dean, Rachel and Phoebe you may have caused me significant pain. However, seeking revenge didn't bring Einstein back nor fill me with long-lasting happiness. In reality, I'm worse off now than where I began. They were wrong for what they did, though two wrongs don't make a right.

CHAPTER 23

Savings Savings

Birthdays are usually a cause for celebration. It's the only day you're allowed to act like a brat and be immune from blame. Unfortunately, with my friendships blossoming, guilt patrolled my life like the moon on a clear night. I never anticipated we would become allies. I've come to understand the choices I make can have monumental impacts. I'd squashed my competition, but at what cost?

'Birthday boy, up and at them!' Mom burst into my bedroom, holding a gift behind her back.

'Sorry son. I told her to ask if you're decent,' said dad, bringing in breakfast: three soft boiled eggs joined by lightly buttered soldiers and fresh apple juice. Traditions are traditions.

'Thanks, dad.'

'I won't ask permission to enter rooms I own.'

'Kids of Oscar's age need space. Remember the conversation we had?'

Mom's reaction suggested she'd been quite repulsed by whatever father referred to.

'All kids go through that phase. It's nature, the boy's animal instinct,' shrugged dad.

'Anyway, presents,' said mom.

Birthday number twelve sat among my very worst, which includes tonsillitis at eight and an appendix removal for my tenth.

Nevertheless, I opened my numerous gifts. I received two hundred and fifty pounds in cash, a further hundred in vouchers and a brand-new mobile phone.

'Eat up, son. Sure your friends have got something special planned for you,' said mom, kissing my cheek.

I dipped the toast into the yolk. My conscience occupied my day. I needed a person to confide in who wouldn't automatically judge. Captivated Lance, still desiring a live nude model, begged his parents to travel to Oxford for an art festival. Maybe a walk could clear my thoughts. Healthy body leads to a healthy mind. I took four strides outside Winterberry before I heard my name.

'Oscar!'

His voice now registered easily. Dean raced over. Is he stalking me?

'I am glad to see you, buddy. Happy birthday mate.'

I sort of half smiled. 'No football with you.'

'Football and I are definitely finito,' he bitterly replied.

However, I knew it was a dishonest statement. As we passed a park Dean surveyed the football scene like a dog when he sees the mailman. His eyes dimmed as players shifted from box to box.

'Who cares? Good luck to them,' Dean said defeated, practically crying.

'What do you want to do today?' I asked.

'Never bothered these days; nothing takes my fancy. As long as I'm away from my rotten sisters. Yesterday they tried to make me wear a dress.'

'Tried to?'

'I resisted with all my worth.'

Dean's siblings got what they wanted when they wanted. So believe you me, Deano wore a dress.

'I got a gift for you back home, Oscar.'

'Really? You shouldn't have gone out of your way,' I explained as my burden ever grew.

'Mom urged me to.'

We walked the narrow streets and winding roads to Dean's home. There he presented me with a gift both caring and hurtful.

'Speak mate, you don't like it?'

'Actually, it's extravagantly excellent.'

'Dad had it framed,' said Dean.

That's just what I needed; a large picture of me and Dean holding a Bass.

'This is spectacular,' I spoke in discomfort.

'Rachael and Phoebe also made you a beaded bracelet.'

I slipped it onto my wrist, staring at the interlinked red, white and blue.

'Phoebe couldn't manage the threading process, so Rachael constructed it.'

'Catch you on the flip side, Dean.'

'Leaving already?' Dean inquired.

'Tired mate, woke up early. Overpowered with excitement.'

I rapidly wandered home, disappointed in my actions. Home hurt too. Mom made from scratch a birthday cake with twelve flickering candles.

'Make a wish, Oscar,' she yelled.

I blew hard but three candles still burnt bright. Did they represent three friends I'm burning right now?

Since mother had questioned dad's duties as a man, he'd bought every power tool under the sun. Glue guns, nail guns, screwdrivers, power saws and jack hammers were all stored in our garage. One glance at my picture frame and he shot straight for the electric screwdriver, drilling my gift to the bedroom wall. Thanks a lot dad.

'Any other services you need, bleeding radiators, fixing a flat tyre or changing locks, come see me,' he bragged.

The picture stayed crooked and was only held up by four baby screws. My sleeping pattern was completely interrupted. I'd like to say it's because of dad's dodgy D.I.Y feebly hanging above the bed. But no, Phoebe's beaded bracelet left an impression on my wrist. A constant reminder. I felt it necessary to seek a cure to their suffering.

That Sunday morning, rattled with guilt, I briskly walked to the canal. Ducks kept an envious eye on me; a few approached the footpath, quacking. Today I brought bread as a peace offering. They accepted my apology gratefully. I came to a standstill near Sam's home.

'Sam, it's Oscar.'

I waited calmly. Then a few leaves parted and out came Sam, all jubilant.

'Hop through lad, bit nippy out here,' he said, throwing on a dusty jacket.

We stepped into his base. He sat on a few pillows, thrilled to hear why I returned.

'Say it like it is. How did your treats produce?'

'They worked wonders.'

'Eureka, who we targeting now?' he beamed.

'Nobody. In fact, I require an antidote. I'm ruining people's lives for eternity. Please take me to see Mrs Doovoo,' I grovelled.

Disappointment stirred inside Sam. I had lost his respect.

'I told you so. Revenge, who needs it? Soon you've cooled off and feel depressed.'

'We've become close friends and I'm going insane, utterly steeped in shame.'

Sam opened a can of spaghetti hoops, dumping the load into a saucepan.

'Fancy some, son?' he asked.

The silver tin reflected its best before date of March 2009. I obviously declined.

'Mrs Doovoo is a trick lady. She is chock-a-block until mid-February. You'll have to wait your turn.'

'I shall return in February,' I said, distressed.

'Hold it. There's an additional fee of one thousand pounds cash up front.'

Knowing full well what had to be done, I set about gaining a steady income. I picked up a double paper round. The going was tough; a hundred papers in the morning followed by a further hundred that evening. I  delivered come rain or shine, through thick fog and harshly cold days Monday to Sunday. Nobody said it was gonna be easy. Then again, the things most wanted usually aren't. Wisely at Christmas I requested money to bolster my funds. Sometimes I skipped meals at school to save lunch money. I could stand to lose a few. After pinching and scrimping, by early February I'd accumulated the relevant dough.

So, at midnight Sam and I met up to visit Mrs Doovoo. Her mood had soured since our previous meeting; refunds damaged her public image.

'If it isn't the boy who wishes for redemption,' she said in a disgusted manner.

'He acted on impulse, not actually understanding his own character,' clarified Sam, placing my brown envelope in her coat pocket.

'I'm being squashed under the weight of burden. All I wanted was to break their hold.'

'Ask and you shall receive,' she replied, counting out my notes into piles of fives, tens and twenties.

'You stole away the one thing they held sacred: art, performing and football.'

Mrs Doovoo didn't welcome my finger pointing. A cold blizzard raced through my body when she gazed at me.

162

'Sam, never waste valuable time on such babies. Actions have consequences. People must treat others how they want to be treated.'

'I'm unquestionably sorry for all this brouhaha. Your potions and remedies are ingenious but I'm not worthy. Please, all I ask for is a quick fix.'

She locked away the loot in a safety deposit box. 'A quick fix? It's more complicated than that. After a certain stage their minds alter.'

'Meaning?' I worried.

Mrs Doovoo flicked through a calendar to assess when her poison first took effect. 'They may be too far gone. By now have they abandoned their broken equipment?'

'Within days,' I said.

'Your friends are in crisis mode. They're suffering from identity failure. Once they begin believing what's in front of them there's almost no hope.'

'Say it ain't so,' I cried.

Mrs Doovoo viewed my distress with a level of compassion. 'Cheer up, chuck.'

'In the confusion of hate I've ruined three people's lives. I'll have to reveal the truth behind their inability to flourish,' I listlessly crawled towards the door.

'A confession,' yelled Mrs Doovoo.

'What?'

'A true confession detailing your reasons could lift the curse. However, forgiveness is hard to come by.'

CHAPTER 24

The Comeback

I've been told it's better to be two steps ahead than one behind. So, at school I summoned Phoebe, Rachael and Dean for clear the air talks. The three worse for wear children were floored; unpopularity had already come, saw and conquered.

'You're not our friend any more. It's the picture frame, right? Stupid me, I just wanted someone to like me,' Dean slapped himself repeatedly.

'It's my face! They're thinking of fitting me with a mask,' frowned Rachael.

'No, the loom band, you're not keen on the colours. What your favourite? I'll make one specifically and unique to you, Oscar,' Phoebe dived into her rucksack. Art supplies shot along the corridor.

'I thought you quit?' asked Dean, helping her collect her gel pens.

'I'm still addicted; ideas flow like sprawling rivers into oceans. Once production moment arrives, I fluff my lines,' she brawled.

'I did this to you, guys,' I blurted.

Saying it aloud relieved me of a mountain of stress. The monkey was off my back.

'Please, Oscar, don't blame yourself. Trying to make excuses. This is who we are. We'll learn to accept it,' Phoebe spoke gently.

'Look, after Einstein's death I went crazy. Irate with anger, hated your guts. I sought vengeance. In my haste I met a conjurer whose name I won't mention. She offered me three tonics to trample those who caused my uneasiness.'

Rachael and Dean awkwardly persisted in silence. Phoebe, the loose cannon, snapped the lid off her gel pen.

'I'll kill him! I'll kill him!'

Dean and Rachael blocked her violent swipes. I earned a few vicious pen marks on my neck. Considering I demolished a touching painting dedicated to her deceased mother we'll call it all square.

Rachael escorted her to the ladies' room.

She seethed in venom. 'Let me at him. I know a secure place to dump the body.'

'You must've expected that reaction. My girl's quite intimately linked to art,' said Dean, relatively calm.

'How do you feel about it?'

'Mean Dean Jackson would've put you through a wall.'

In boxing seventy-five per cent of rematches wind up with similar results to the original bout. I bore that in mind.

'And now?'

'I still want to put you through a wall,' he growled, balling up his fists.

'But!'

'We're amigos. Old savage Dean doesn't live or belong here,' he claimed.

'Right on. Plus, your footballing craft should recover.'

Dean smirked; his eyes widened in glee like he'd found a bundle of cash.

'I can play the game. I CAN PLAY THE GAME.'

Without Dean in the line-up Winterberry's year 7s title challenge had tailed off. They now prop up the rear of the table, eighteen points adrift of Moss Town. But a cup romance sent them to the quarter finals against hotly tipped Platinum Grammar School, Timothy's new team.

'I'm so happy I could kiss you.'

He didn't.

At lunch Rachael's porridge texture was beginning to turn custardy – not thick and yellow but glossy and smooth. Her bald spot had grown back rapidly. Guys fell off chairs and missed their mouths when eating in their admiration of her.

'So maybe my personality wasn't on par with my looks,' she stroked her beautiful hair. 'It took someone to humble me in order to find a balance between glamour and grace. I solely thank you.'

She charmingly kissed my cheek. Oscar "the Lothario" Smart. I'll take it.

'We'll hang out later, Romeo,' she winked.

Lads from years 7 to 11, sixth form, caretakers, dinner men and on duty teachers converged on my table.

'Teach us,' they pestered.

I shrugged. 'Go with the flow.'

Everyone scrambled to write my quote.

Dean's ex-brilliant bunch demonstrated their intelligence.

'Flow with the flow he said.'

'No. I'm positive it's go with the go.'

'Let's jot down both to avoid mistakes.'

Winterberry High never seemed so enjoyable. Mr Russell demanded The Haunted One's demolition. Mr Trent, still hunting for a healing treatment, travelled to Holland. So long Sweaty Betty. With his disappearance arts became my lone problematic subject. Noting Phoebe's daily decline really sucked. But like an old pair of socks, she found her feet. When on top of their game all performers have quirky habits. Phoebe tilted her head, cocking the tongue out to the left. She lightly shaded and blended. There was a distinct reversal in her attitude. An expression of elation spread with each dash of her pencil.

'I'm embracing my flair. The visions are dazzling,' said a merry Phoebe.

'You're an artist in heart, body and soul,' praised our teacher, giving Phoebe the customary A*.

'Well done Phoebs,' exalted classmates.

'I have a special friend to thank for my revival,' she hailed. (This actually didn't play out so comfortably. In fact, it took endless months of apologies, a heartfelt message over Tongue Wagger before we were even on speaking terms. All's good know though.)

'You're welcome.'

She nodded, suggesting all was forgiven.

Free from my sins, I sailed through final period science and attention turned to the beautiful game. Dean's practice session had sent nattering fans manic. The sight of those golden boots caressing a football was sheer heaven. The posh toffs from Platinum Grammar School filed out of one bedecked coach filled with exclusive facilities like personal fridges, projection monitor, spa and built in Wi-Fi. Their kits were silky purple and by you'll never guess who bought them. The Nation of Sugar, who in return displayed his logo from top to toe. Each starlet required their own assistants, whose single job was to see these super athletes didn't overheat, carry their own luggage or open doors.

The game was played in fair conditions; none of those rough-house tactics. Platinum Grammar kept the ball well. They adopted technical short, easy tiki-taka passing. Their sharp one touch football had us scrambling to plug gaps.

'Tuck in. Jockey him, James, eye on the ball,' shouted coach.

A couple of speculative efforts stung our goalkeeper's palm. It was more when rather than if they'd break the stalemate.

Dean, not totally match fit, sat on the bench restlessly. 'Coach, tag me in. I've highlighted a weakness at full back. Let me exploit him.'

'Halftime, if we're still nil-nil. Remember we got a relegation dogfight to contend with.'

'But coach, they'll score from their next set piece. Our defence is being run ragged,' he judged, signalling for the defenders to push out.

Unfortunately, one cumbersome player ignored the guidance; this left him one v one with their lethal striker. Dumbstruck, he made the only available play, tugging the shirt. Easy call. The referee blew for a free kick near the halfway line. Their centre half lofted a ball into the eighteen-yard box; a frantic scramble ensued and eventually the ball trickled in.

'Coach! Put me on, they need leading,' begged Dean.

Just before the ref concluded the first forty-five a misplaced backpass caused danger. Platinum Grammar's lightning no.9 latched on, rounding the keeper and slotting home to double their advantage.

Timothy screamed, relishing the glory. 'Can't buy a win these days, Oscar.'

After half time oranges we expected more of the onslaught. Platinum Grammar strung a stunning thirty-three pass sequence together, culminating with a third.

'Go for four,' Timothy chanted.

At the sixty-minute mark double figures was on their radar.

'Dean, stretch your legs,' instructed the Coach.

'Unleash me,' he gleamed.

'Ref, sub.'

Dean wandered on. Players examined his posture; the pumped-up chest and face burning with determination wobbled Platinum's defender.

'Keep it tight, no space,' yelled Platinum's manager.

When you're stuck up a creek without a paddle you either sink or swim.

'We're playing for pride lads, now c'mon,' rallied Dean.

Platinum sat back, ready to break on a slick counter. Their zippy winger lost possession cutting inside. A swift toe poke down the byline and Dean retrieved the ball, creating hysteria.

'Go on son!' I blared.

Two players came to thwart his progress. One pivot, two ste-povers and a nutmeg later Dean sped off. Defenders tumbled, unsure whether to stick or twist. He glided by both awestruck oppo-nents, then audaciously chipped the converging goalie. Three one.

'Keep going, no quitting! Fight! Every second is vital,' Dean prompted.

Seeing him thrive in his natural habitat made me reflect on what I nearly permanently stole. A fifty-yard ball Dean brought under his spell instantly. He dropped the shoulder, injecting dynamic pace. Defenders trailed until one burly midfielder hacked him at the knees.

'Foul ref.'

The referee agreed, awarding a free-kick centrally thirty yards from goal. Dean planted the ball with purpose.

'Yards! No way are they ten yards,' he shouted, clearing lumps of mud out of his studs.

'Shuffle back guys,' said the referee.

The wall edged back two yards. Their goalkeeper positioned it in front of the ball.

Dean, an expert from dead ball situations, stepped up and curled a peach of shot into the top corner. The goalkeeper stood rooted without a prayer of saving it. Winterberry's lads snatched the ball, convinced they were destined to come back. Panicked

Platinum boys delayed, faking injuries or huddling up in the corner. Minutes fled towards the ninety and a few half chances went begging. Dean grappled with two chaperone defenders. His rousing impact dwindled in the closing stages and tiredness kicked in. A snappy one-two with his strike partner released him. He spanked the ball's base, maximising its force; a clean sighted goalie tipped it over. Last roll of the dice, a corner kick. My heart fluttered anxiously. A deep inward swinging cross arrived, the goalkeeper fully committed in no man's land. A rash clearance falls to our right back and he launches it forward; rising above it all for his hattrick, Dean Jackson. The bullet header nestles in the onion bag. Three all. Extra time, surely.

'Put that in you pipe and smoke it, Timothy,' I gloated.

Mass confusion surrounded the fans, players and staff. The referee pointed for a free kick instead of kicking off from the centre circle.

'Offside, you're having a laugh,' moaned coach.

Players argued, but Platinum Grammar proceeded to the semi.

The dreaded offside rule. Offside occurs when a player is behind the last line of defence as a teammate makes the pass.

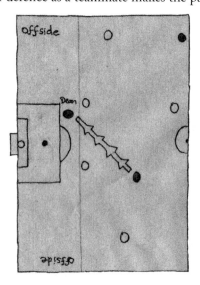

CHAPTER 25

Walking in a Winterberry Land

My life had come full circle from something to nothing to something again. The dark days never last; you just have to stay positive and wait for the shining light to break through. I was in a happy place. Mother and father were rekindling their romance. Dad received a promotion with a mighty bump in pay. He wined and dined mother with a shopping spree to New York, two weeks all expenses paid. While she was away remastering her wardrobe, father ignited plans to renovate the entire house. He decided to hire outside help.

As it transpired Dean's father was a professional builder with twenty years of experience. And now Dean was firmly a friend of mine, we got special mate's rates. Jimmy gutted our pad, tearing down decaying walls and ceiling panels. Huge earth movers dug up the cracked driveway. Patchy roof slates were also removed. Dust, smoke, fumes and chemicals engulfed our home. Money man father opened his wallet, springing for a five-star hotel. Room service, mini bar and heated indoor swimming pool, what more could a boy want?

Jimmy was so competent in his trade he even allowed father to help. Provided he was supervised. To fit in dad got a hi-viz vest, hard hat and tool belt which stocked moisturiser, aftershave and mouthwash. Glamour Puss they labelled him.

'Being around the lads on a building site, getting your hands filthy, mixing cement, plastering walls, climbing scaffolding. It's a job and a half,' he blabbed.

'Sounds like you've had an entertaining time of it.'

'I tell you, Oscar, stripping down old beams, nailing plaster-boards, smacking in wall insulation. Sanding, sawing, hacking boosts my macho rankings,' said an animated dad.

'Try to sleep dad, it's four in the morning.'

'Sleep, I want to build, construct and produce,' he again exalted, reading a building magazine.

Day by day he'd unveil a new story of what recent method he learnt. You're never too old to be taught. One week on from their commencement the structure was finished and built like a brick . . . house. Pricey grey slates replaced old dainty dull ones, and solar panels were mounted too. Somebody's gotta protect the environment. The patio displayed wonderful crazy paving. Ceilings

172

and walls lay parallel to one another. They added a front porch too with double glazing.

Running water in our house had been a considered luxury; drains regurgitated sewer waste. Phoebe and I developed a strong bond which served remarkably, because her father owned a plumbing company. Within a two-day period, he'd used microscopic cameras to snake down drainpipes into the main body of our underground system.

'Whoever lived here before you flushed dozens of full disposable nappies. There's a healthy clogging,' he declared.

'That's what I calculated myself. Stuck in the U-bend,' agreed Dad.

'The U-bend's completely clear, Mr Smart. Please put down the wrench, sir.'

Dad glanced at him, perturbed; his manicured fingers loosened the silver wrench.

'If you're gonna assist you'll need to be kitted out. What size are you, large?' smiled Phoebe's father.

'A medium. I do yoga; helps strengthen the core,' explained dad, not understanding guy code.

Talk sports, women, cars, bikes; how you much can drink or eat. Anything else shut it.

Anyway, supposedly dad aided them, making mugs of tea. Soon copper pipes connected to a boiler transferring fresh, fluid hot water to pleasure us.

Electronics caused its share of headaches. In the kitchen and lounge two appliances couldn't be in use at once or a blackout would manifest. What a coinkydink Rachael's dad's occupation was as an electrician. Rachael and I were sort of dating; don't wanna rock the boat. Dean halted me from bellowing it to everyone over the tannoy. But, between us, Rachael and Oscar sitting in a tree k-i-s-s-i-n-g . . . ah you know the rest. Mother hadn't accepted there was another lady love in my life. Nonetheless, her father who I'm still struggling to win over, rewired the home effortlessly.

'Electrics are extremely hazardous, Oscar,' he said imposingly.

'I know, sir,' I replied.

Sparks were fizzing out a live wire.

'A wrong wire here or there, put a fuse in incorrectly and fire-works, explosion then ultimately death. Understand, Oscar? Never be careless with the fuse,' he grunted, squeezing my shoulder.

'Fuses are not toys. Got it,' I winced.

'Don't fiddle with my electrics. If you do, I'll be back, unhappy, and my positives will outweigh your negatives.'

He let go of my bruised shoulder. A hunch told me he wasn't speaking of circuit breakers, high voltage or fuse boxes.

'Zap!' he yelled.

'Jeepers,' I squirmed, rattled.

'Scare you? I never meant to pylon.'

Atrocious wordplay.

'You're too funny,' I chuckled.

'Remember, volts and amps.'

His steely glare lingered for days. I switched on plugs using clothes gloves.

Further changes followed. Firstly, after dad's motor resound-ingly failed its M.O.T due to a broken suspension, electrical fault, dodgy exhaust and shredded handbrake cable, as well as needing a new head gasket, he scrapped the orange piece of trash for a very noble British Jaguar and actually selected the brash supercharged V8 model. We christened it by surging down the motorway to pick mom up from Gatwick. As law-abiding people, we respected the seventy-mph restriction, honestly. Mother wheeled a suitcase containing half of the Big Apple. However, a fully loaded boot didn't diminish the Jag's pulling power.

'How are my two favourite people in the universe?' she asked.

'Blissful, mom,' I gleamed.

Dad pressed a button, making the panoramic sunroof trans-parent and inviting luscious, dazzling stars to twinkle. Allured, Mr Moon joined in the celebration; they all glistened and sparkled throughout the night sky.

'You've both been busy bees,' said a shocked mother, gawking at our restoration project.

'Man's gotta do what he's gotta do,' said dad, opening the front door, 'P.V.C frame. Mayflower glass; they tell me it's shatterproof. Next month Oscar and I are gonna build a gazebo.'

'News to me,' I responded, slightly worried.

Dad gripped my forearm. 'Son, since my departure from Sugar Nation we don't share a common interest. I thought father and son could combine to erect a sensational structure.'

As time went by, we had partly become more roommates than parent and child. It might have been a guilt trip, but definitely achieved its purpose.

'Dreaming of the prospect, dad.'

He grinned; those bleached white teeth radiated like switching on a zillion watt light bulb.

Mother furnished our home from top to bottom.

Believe it or not father, without any professional direction, forged a quite magnificent gazebo. We worked together on weekends and he knew every technique, technical term and did the ghastly deed of wolf whistling at mother as she brought lunch.

'How's it going, darling?' he said in builder's slang.

She became flustered in affection for her handyman.

He was so proud, he saved a picture of it as his phone's wall-paper. 'Craftsmanship at its finest.'

The world keeps spinning and life waits for no one. Father earned the megabucks again. Including bonuses, he averaged Sugar Nation's kind of coin. Since our bumpy introduction, Winterberry lost its shock value. Roads lay bare and gentle. Kids played in parks. Neighbours chatted over fences free of egos and jealously. I was gathering a host of information, a social education on how people survive below the poverty line. My personal growth over the last twelve months was bigger than that of my first eleven years.

Congratulations you've made it to the end. Thanks for reading and I'll see you in the not so distant future.

Congratulations you've made it to the end. Thanks for reading and I'll see you in the not so distance future.

Printed in Great Britain
by Amazon

46795785R00106